ONL`

Tom Burton

Hope you enjoy these stories!

T Burton

First published in Great Britain in 2022

Copyright © Tom Burton 2022

Typeset in Garamond

ISBN: 979-8-50324-530-1

CONTENTS

ÖTZI

'Please don't leave,' she begs.

'I'll only be away for a few days,' he assures her, reaching over to brush back a stray lock of her hair. 'I'll be back before the next moonrise.'

She doesn't reply; she knows this journey will end him.

She sees in her dreams the fatal blow from behind, the arrow shot by an unseen enemy. It will happen in the middle of the night, far from her. She sees it on the first night they spend together, her stomach curdled with dread, but he chuckles when she warns him. He rises from their rumpled bed of warm scratchy furs, roars 'Who is this enemy? Come out and face me!' and beats away shadows and phantoms. He presses a hairy hand to his broad chest, rolls his eyes and whines like a grizzling newborn. 'Help me, I'm scared!' he groans in mock terror, then wraps her in his brawny arms and peppers her face with kisses until his tickling beard finally makes her squeal and giggle.

1

Her dreams can wait. At least for tonight.

Later, they lie together in a warm tangle of limbs as she idly traces a finger over the hard scarred expanse of his muscular torso. His chest is dark-pelted, broad and taut as calfskin, his tanned forehead creased with wrinkles; he is her bedmate, lover, protector and defender, thick-limbed and unashamed of his rough brawler's reputation.

It won't save him. The fear returns, creeping over her like a chill morning frost. 'Please don't go,' she pleads again.

He squeezes her hand, tenderly stroking his thumb over her knuckles. 'I have to,' he murmurs. 'Goats need herding. Spring thaw's here soon. I'll bring back an ibex for you.' His gaze drifts over her swollen belly. 'For both of you. Good idea?'

She turns over with a tired sigh. From outside their tent flap echoes the familiar sounds of camp. A gruff bark of laughter. The soft patter of feet dashing past. Children giggling. A mother crooning to her gurgling babe. The steady *tock! tock!* of clansmen knapping flint flakes.

He'll be leaving all the warm comforts of home. She can't dissuade him, or his twitchy eagerness to depart like a wolf that's caught a fresh scent. Still, he has an inborn sadness that even she can't cure; the aching twinges in his limbs after recent snowfall, the sudden stomach pains that leave him groaning and hunched over despite the mushrooms he chews, his wheezing coughs that often keep her up half the night. Even as his beard thickens and her belly swells further, his spirit is waning.

He needs this journey. He travels not because he knows languages or is a tribal elder, but because the icy mountain air clears his lungs and the familiar repetition of walking soothes him.

Next morning she stitches his sheepskin parka and finishes sewing his bearskin cap, fills his travelling pouch with dried mushrooms and carves her sign into the ash hilt of his flint knife. A piece of her with him, wherever he roams.

He pulls on his red deer jerkin, then his thick winter boots, the ones she'd painstakingly repaired only two nights ago, their tough bearskin soles perfect for trekking over icy rock, the soft goatskin leggings packed with grass for warmth and comfort.

He is cloaked from head to toe in animal pelts, both those they raise and those he hunts. Perhaps this blend of familiar and strange hides will help protect him on his journey.

Perhaps.

She packs and repacks his larch and hazel-wood backpack, fretting with anxiety until he chuckles and gently takes her hands, his rough callused paws swallowing her slender brown fingers. 'Honestly, I'll be *fine*,' he insists, showing her the bone needles and deer-sinew thread, the smouldering charcoal embers and tinder fungus wrapped in maple leaves for his birchbark canisters.

'What if your stomach pains come back? Have you got your –'

'Yes. Got plenty of those.' He pats the necklace of walnut-sized birch mushrooms around his neck, then pulls her close and presses a fond kiss to her brow. 'Honestly, it'll be *fine*. And if anyone tries anything funny –' he pats the copper-bladed axe tucked into his belt, then his leaf-shaped knife as jagged and sharp as a wolf's jaw – 'they'll get a nasty surprise.'

She sees how other strangers will find him one day, entombed in ice. How his fame will sprout and grow until it is enormous, revered, god-like among men. He will be regarded as a mystery; he will fascinate generations yet unborn.

Of course, she doesn't tell him this. No need to swell his ego any further.

The clan sees him off at dawn, clustered together before their humped deerskin shelters, hands raised in farewell as he clambers up the mountainside. He turns at the next jagged summit, puffs out his chest and roars a jubilant cry to the camp below. Then he hurries off along the ridge. Disappears from view.

Come back to us, she pleads silently. *Come back to me.*

She knows he is still a boy at heart, the same brash lad who scraped his knees rock-climbing, wept in her arms afterwards, and gifted her a perfect white flower like a starburst of new-fallen snow. She nurtures that memory for herself, cradles it, nourishes it. He will be singing of her every night, as he promised, even on the fatal night he finally falls.

Her breasts ache with milk, swollen and heavy. She knows she will not survive to see the strange men unearth his body from the ice. Nobody lives that long. The baby shifts inside her, kicking with impatience, a fighter eager to come into the world. *Just like you, my love*, she thinks. *If it's a boy, let him have your rich, booming laugh and fearless strength. If it's a girl, let her have your gentle hands, your dark brown eyes, your beaming smile like dawning sunlight.*

She will never see him again. The dread certainty sinks its claws into her belly. She will continue on her own journey upon the woman-path, the journey of blood, sweat and pain that stays in place yet runs continuously like a roaring river. He

5

will never see their child brought bloody and wailing into this harsh world of ice and rock. But she will sing her song for him, every day for the rest of her life, until the darkness takes her in turn and she joins him among the stars.

WAVES AND WISDOM

It is a glorious spring afternoon, and King Canute is hating every minute of it.

Good or bad, a king attracts flatterers like a horse attracts flies, and in his vast fenland kingdom Canute has accumulated a veritable swarm of sycophants. Even now as he toils at his desk, signing proclamations and scribbling messages, their honeyed words pour over him.

'The sun is shining today, my lord, because it is so glad to see you so well!'

Canute's quill scratches. 'Indeed.'

'The kings of all Europe are trembling this morning, your honour, at the thought of your might and wisdom!'

Canute bites back a growl of irritation. 'Highly unlikely, I'm sure.' In hindsight, he probably should have made his throne room smaller. The Great Hall is grand enough for receptions and royal feasts, impressing foreign nobles and flaunting his grandeur – it's not everyday you meet a man who rules three separate seafaring kingdoms combined. But there's a roaring open fire in the centre of the vast room that he cannot feel, and even the two flaming braziers flanking his throne don't warm him either.

His mind begins to idly wander; Emma will be upstairs in their bedroom, maidservants by her side as she combs her long brown tresses, humming with the morning lark. Harthacnut will be over in the banqueting hall, playfully brawling with the fireside dogs like any nine-year-old lad.

'The Pope himself is surely envious of your saintliness, my liege!'

Canute straightens up in his chair. 'I daresay I could cross swords with the moon and win.'

'Oh, no doubt! No question, my lord King!'

Canute's eyes narrow. 'And command the sea to do my bidding, hm?'

'The seas, my lord King, would be honoured to serve you,' another toady simpers.

The king stands up. 'Then take hold of my throne – you – you – you – and you! – and be so good as to carry it down to the beach. Well? Come on!'

He steps down from his dais into a sea of startled stares and scatters his council, courtiers bowing and parting like the Red Sea before him. Canute strides past them, head high as he hastens out the palace throne room towards the main gate, flanked by his armed escort. The courtiers straggle behind bleating in protest, four of them puffing and straining as they lug his carved oaken throne. Fat lazy sluggards! Canute smiles to himself; his palace guards trot alongside, easily keeping pace despite the heavy weight of their chainmail hauberks, helmets and boots.

The palace courtyard is alive with bustling activity. A horse whinnies from the stables. The steady clink of metalwork from the blacksmith's forge. A kitchen boy ambles past, herding a squabbling gaggle of geese with a stick. He gawps at the curious procession.

Canute smiles back. 'Move along! Nothing to see here!' More guards watch from the walled stockade as he crosses the defensive ditch, followed by his trailing entourage.

The marshes of Thorney Island stretch down to the wide flowing tidal river. On his left Canute sees several black-robed Benedictine monks meander inside the tall monastery of West Minster, their melodic Latin chants fading on the breeze.

Soon they pass through the whispering marshes and arrive on a gently sloping beach. The estuary lies vast and grey before them, breathing shallowly, lapping at shells on the sodden sand. Canute has his throne placed at the water's edge and sits. His courtiers mill about, hands clasped over their stomachs, smiles set hard. The tide is rising.

'Hold off, sea!' Canute commands, holding up a regal palm. 'I, Canute, say you shall not rise today!' His courtiers glance at each other, but continue smiling nervously even as the surf creeps closer.

'Stay back, thou great wet thing!' Canute protests, now holding up both royal hands. 'I, Canute, command you: cease your advance!'

But of course, the sea continues to lap the shore, and every seventh wave hisses higher up the beach, wetting dry sand, turning dry pebbles. Soon the legs of the gold-gilded throne are awash. The royal feet are distinctly wet. Hopping about dismally, the courtiers continue smiling.

'O unruly proud monster! Do you defy me? Do you dare invade my kingdom?' A large grey wave soaks everyone to the knees and the backwash drags sand from under their sodden velvet shoes.

The chancellor lurches forward, drenched in seaspray. 'I really think, your Majesty,' he bleats, 'it's not quite safe to …'

'But you told me I was more powerful than the ocean itself!' Canute retorts and settles back on his throne, steadfast even as his throne is rocked by large cold waves and his courtiers are now up to their waists in brine.

'Scurvy ocean!' Canute yells. 'I see that you have not yet heard of King Canute the All-Powerful!' He rises up from his throne, hands balled into fists. 'I see that we must wrestle hand-to-hand!'

'No! No, my lord!' cry several of his courtiers, flailing through the swell towards him. 'Don't! Please!'

'You mean to say I am *not* all-powerful?' Canute replies with exaggerated amazement. 'You mean to say that the winds and waves do *not* obey God's anointed sovereign?'

'I, ah –'

'We –'

'Erm –'

'No? Then hear this!' He wades ashore amid the incoming tide. 'Let all men know that the power of kings is vain and worthless, and that none is worthy of the name of king save Lord God Almighty, He whose eternal laws command heaven, earth and sea. Is that understood?'

As one, his councillors fall to their knees in the churning surf. 'Yes, your Majesty!' Every head is bowed in humbled servitude.

Well … almost everyone. His guards are leaning on their spears, openly grinning at the sorry spectacle of grovelling courtiers before him. Canute bites back a smile, fixing his face in a stern glare of reproach.

A king must keep up appearances, after all.

'Any more vain excuses? No? Then in future, gentlemen, I'll thank you not to tell me such monumental untruths. I look to you for your help, advice and measured opinions – *not* for flattery, fawning lies and pathetic servility. Do I make myself clear?'

'Perfectly!' howls the court in unison as a great foaming wave crashes down and leaves them stumbling ashore, drenched and gasping and dipping for their hats in the vast unheeding sea.

Canute turns to watch a flock of seagulls swirl across the whispering marshland, their shrill chorus fading on the breeze. And suddenly, the echo of the waves hissing over beach pebbles sounds like a ripple of welcome applause.

TORCHBEARER

Let me tell you about Tyndale. Who am I? Nobody much. In fact, better if I don't tell you my name, or else I'll be in trouble with the authorities again. But to me, Tyndale was one of the greatest men who ever lived.

And now they've burned him. Like a log of wood, they've burned him.

He studied at Oxford and Cambridge; a brilliant scholar – he could even speak five languages! His colleagues had naught but praise to sing about him. But when he set about translating the New Testament from Latin to English, for the common people to read, suddenly he was a criminal. Had to flee abroad to carry on his work.

Even across the Narrow Sea they hunted him everywhere, hounded from house to house. Some villain overheard the printers gushing about this new book they were working on: Tyndale's New Testament. 'What a revolution this will stir up in England!' the printers rejoiced, and this skulking eavesdropper thought: revolution? Here's news the authorities will want to hear about.

When they raided the printers and broke down the door, only the first ten sheets had been run off, ink barely dry. But William was too quick for them. He'd had those ten sheets rolled up inside his pack, and was already far away across the Low Countries to another city, long before they could ever lay hands on him. A weary pilgrim on the lonesome road, walking through the wilderness like Elijah to the mountain of God. Nourished by his faith.

He was in danger the whole time, a wanted fugitive hunted every day of every year, always looking over his shoulder. But he pressed on. Two editions were finally printed – one large leather-bound tome for reading aloud in public, one small enough to fit into a man's pocket, or hold in your own hands. Anyone's hands. Yours. Mine.

He needed help to distribute them, naturally. European merchants regularly crossed the Channel to and fro, Tyndale's little printed Bibles hidden among their goods as seaspray lashed the decks. Bales of linen. Casks of grain. Soon they were selling for just two shillings each in shady corners and at secret back-alley doors. Over six thousand in the country before the bishops even knew what was happening. Everyone wanted one. *I* wanted one. I don't ever remember hungering after a thing so much, or prizing anything so dearly as that small brown parcel slipped into my hand one rainy day, in a shadowy porch on Sheep Street.

Thomas More labelled us heathen swine. Bishop Stokesley, London's scourge of heretics, brands us Satan's shit and godless heretics. Bishop Tunstall breathes hellfire on us from his lofty Durham pulpit. Stephen Gardiner, Bishop of Winchester, sneers that Tyndale's Bible is an ignorant smear of blasphemy riddled with errors. Doesn't matter. What did a few silly errors matter to the likes of us commoners who had always been shut out from understanding, because nobody bothered to teach us Latin? Excuses. Just another feeble excuse for them to hoard God all to themselves – not share him about. "Pearls trampled under the feet of swine," all the clever scholars and bishops bleated. Let them hold their monopoly of Latin, the exclusive privilege of nobles, popes, clerics and kings. We don't care. Here's the Word of God in our hands at last, in our own language. God speaks to you as your own mother and father spoke, as your wet nurse: even if you can't read, others will read it for you, in this loving, close, familiar tongue.

When they couldn't track down the printing

presses, they bought up thousands of finished copies and burned them in great public bonfires. But the more books they burned, the more people whispered, then muttered, then roared: 'What's so important about this? What are you hiding from us?'

So King Henry made it illegal to own a Tyndale Bible.

Troopers searched high and low, in bread ovens and mangers and haylofts. Anyone found owning or reading a New Testament was thrown in prison for a month. I was one.

A grey Strove Tuesday, 1527. There were five of us – four men and a woman. They dressed us all in penitent smocks of sackcloth and gave us candles to carry, bound faggots of wood to our backs. Paraded us barefoot through the streets to the marketplace, showered with mocking jeers and rotten scraps of food. We had to kneel on the cold ground and beg forgiveness from the people for our "crime". Then we were led three times around a bonfire – had to fuel it with those dry faggots – and they made us throw our Bibles into the flames.

Like throwing in my very heart, I can tell you. Hated myself for doing it. Tyndale had given us this great book and here I was, destroying his long years of hard work, apologising for the joy he had freely gifted me, apologising for my wicked crime. Of course I never meant a word of what I said that day. But I still said it, even so. Like the apostle Peter denying Christ three times, to save his own sorry skin. Beside me, my three brothers in Christ gazed blankly into the flames as searing heat washed over our faces. The woman sank to her knees weeping. Behind us stood a smirking monk like a fat grey rat, jewelled cross clutched in his pink paws, eyes glittering as the paper shrivelled and blackened.

And now they've thrown Tyndale himself into the fire. Do you know his last words, after they strangled him at the stake and lit the pyre beneath him? "Oh Lord, open the King of England's eyes." That's what he called out, wrapped in his sheet of blistering flames.

A ghastly public spectacle in Vilvoorde's open marketplace. A warning. *Don't look away. Witness what happens to heretics.* But to their everlasting credit, not one onlooker clapped. Not one voice jeered. Not even the Flemish guards bearing him to the stake, the grim-faced brutes doing their jobs, the ones usually beyond caring. A meek, gentle scholar consigned to the flames. A watchful, unsmiling crowd of dozens, English merchants and Flemish townsfolk alike giving the boldest form of dissent they could manage. Silence. Which roared *we do not agree. We do not condone. All of this is cruel. All of this is wrong.*

Lord knows they've tried their hardest to stamp us out, to scourge us from the earth with fire and steel. For daring to question the Church, for daring to think the Eucharist is only bread and the Blood of Christ is just communion wine, for daring to disbelieve in Purgatory. No longer mindless sheep of the Church's flock. Joan Boughton. Thomas Bilney. John Tewkesbury. James Bainham. John Frith. And now Tyndale himself.

We freethinkers are living on borrowed time, hushed meetings in small back rooms, a bag always packed, a blade concealed close to hand, an ear always alert, one eye on the door; we sleep lightly, and some fitful nights hardly at all.

But they can't burn everyone, and they'll never lock us all up. They have prisons enough for bodies, yes. But an idea? It's impossible to eradicate. Dead men remain hard at work. Their cause is not lost. They labour on from beyond the grave, screened from us by smoke. We could not save Tyndale, but we can save his lifelong work. A light of learning flung far into the future, for countless generations to come.

They can close down the booksellers, but still

there will be books. Let them come looking. We'll confound them. They uncover one hiding place, we'll make another. They can keep their old bones, their cold vaulted halls, their marble saints and gold shrines, their priests and prayers.

But we have the printing press.

They'll never stop this floodtide of faith, never suppress Tyndale's words for good. No chance. With every passing month the old certainties are steadily chipped away – nowhere in holy scripture does it once mention penances or Purgatory, relics or rosary beads. Show us where it says monks or nuns. Is "Pope" in there somewhere? Thought not.

On Tyndale's title page, where the printer's name and address should be, are the words PRINTED IN UTOPIA. Perhaps someone should have sent More a copy on his last night languishing in the Tower. Imagine his face!

For the Holy Church will never win. The French Inquisition tortures heretics and Emperor Charles has women buried alive; they offer their subjects nothing but pain, punishment and fear. And if there is indeed a God, He would never rejoice at the burnings, beheadings and maimings committed in His name. He would celebrate the very best we could be, not condone the worst we are. Men, not monsters. Angels, not beasts. The Church offers people only agony, terror, cruelty and despair. So what, if it has plans for people? Tyndale has dreams for them.

Well, you can burn a man, and you can burn his books. But the truth won't burn, no more than water or milk. Fifty thousand copies have come into this country since the presses started up again in Belgium, seeping into every English parish. You might as well try and gather up all the sand on England's beaches as keep all those books from the people. It can't be done. They might plug one leak into this blessed isle of Albion, but we'll carve out a dozen more. Look here, hidden behind this panel in the wall: here's proof. Take it out. Hold it. Open it. Read it yourself. Go on.

They'll never stop up God's mouth for good – not now He's able to speak to us face to face, in Tyndale's English.

And God said, *Let there be light: and there was light.*

You want to see what freedom looks like? Watch us.

SWANSONG

'Three cheers for the Nine Day Queen! Heh heh!'

'Give us a royal wave, Miss Dudley! Come on!'

She stands at the prow, as still as any carved figurehead, barely a breath of wind to stir her hair as the boat rocks beneath her. The barge bobs sluggishly forward, oars easing through the muddy water. She shuts her eyes. Tries to block out the faint jeers, the mocking hoots and distant catcalls echoing from both riverbanks. No luck. The hecklers are easily keeping pace alongside.

Calm. Certain. Graceful. Dignified. Her mother's encouraging murmurs while adjusting her French hood or brushing out her long auburn hair. The essence of queenship; she must not shrink from her fate, must not falter from her doom set before her. She raises a hand to smooth back an errant curl, masking the tremble of her thin fingers. Her hands drift down to the jewelled Bible on its golden girdle chain at her waist. *Courage, Jane. Courage until the end.*

Henry FitzAlan has moved into Bradgate House, or so her few remaining handmaidens have told her. Mary has ordered him to dissolve the Dudley household. By day, she assumes the Earl of Arundel strides triumphant through deserted oak-panelled rooms, swaggering about, breathing in the lingering aroma of paper and ink, the perfume of rosewater and the sharp tang of linseed. By night his lanky greyhound probably trots across the floor, sniffing the scent of long-dead spaniels and ermines. He wanders the moonlit halls lured along by the boiled meats of a decade of dinners, the bones of scurrying mice furred with dust behind the wainscot, watching an owl's shadow flit past the frosty windowpane.

Henry cannot dissolve my household, she thinks, with a rush of vicious anger. *He can only blunder through the glass and shatter it, bleeding from a thousand cuts. As any turncoat traitor deserves.*

13th September 1553; a raw Friday of splintering cold. It was barely two o'clock in the afternoon when she and her four companions were marched from the riverside quay up to Guildhall. A chill river breeze stinging her cheeks, prickling her arms into gooseflesh.

She bites down a smile at the memory: the pitiful little procession led through a sea of

22

gormless, dull-eyed frowns by an axeman. No real executioner, this, unless executioners were tubby, put-upon little wheezers. The sun shrouded from sight, imprisoned above endless locked grey cloud.

Then a surge of blazing rage: the long droning Latin sermon as she stepped inside the oak-panelled hall, the judges waddling to their seats bedecked in fancy robes, crossing themselves and whispering 'Amen' before they condemned all the guilty men to a long lingering death for high treason. Hanged, drawn and quartered on Tower Hill, slow and leisurely. Exactly like the crucifixion on Calvary. Her beloved friend Thomas Cranmer, Archbishop of Canterbury. Her husband Guildford Dudley. His older brothers Ambrose and Henry.

She still cannot believe it: Archbishop Thomas Cranmer to be butchered for opposing the Catholic mass? Thomas Cranmer, the godly priest who gave England its own *Book of Common Prayer*? That black-clad, silver-bearded man of God who translated the psalms with dear Queen Catherine? Who administered the last rites to dying King Henry and cooled his feverish brow with rosewater? Her mentor? Eviscerated for heresy? How can he be a treasonous heretic? How can his friend's firstborn daughter disembowel such a kindly, gentle-mannered man, after all he has done

23

for this free blessed realm of England?

All those peers of the realm shuffling onto benches to betray her, daydreaming of a speedy return to their fine London residences, to a roaring fire, tankard of ale and slice of game pie. She'd stood stony-faced in the dock and stared them out as their lies and death threats washed over her. All those plump ham-faced traitors who were happy to kneel at her feet during those few precious days when she was Queen, those thirteen fleeting mornings after her cousin croaked his last.

All those wheedling, doddery old greybeards and nodding sycophants who'd crowded the boy-King's sickbay where he lay, bloating and peeling and leaking until he'd shakily signed that document naming her as his rightful successor: splintering his ribs with slimy coughs and vomiting up his stomach lining, all the while the duke by his bedside with that damned piece of parchment, pestering him to *Sign this, why don't you sign this* … Her privy counsellors were eager enough to support her back then, when the wind was in her favour. No hint of disloyalty or false faith, then.

But now? They've all abandoned her. Saw the wind was blowing in Mary's favour, and fled from her side like rats fleeing a sinking ship. Condemned her as a traitor and usurper, a wrongful ascendent to the English throne. Sentenced her to die by either the axe, like a traitor, or fire, like a heretic. Cast her away like a soiled handkerchief, only to be remembered thereafter with a dismissive chortle: *The Grey girl? Oh, the Grey girl! Odd little thing she was, head full of fancies, terribly serious about all this silly nonsense.*

It was not yet four when they cast off from the wooden pier beneath London Bridge, under a cloudless afternoon sky. Vaulted arches of honeyed stone above them, the playful clamour of Southwark priory's bells from the far bank, her whole life receding behind her with every oar stroke. Hours of dazzling daylight left. A workman sitting high on scaffolding, shirtless, pink as a ham from sunburn and whistling 'The Jolly Forester'.

Her husband is weeping between the oarsmen, shrunken, huddled in on himself like a blubbering child. She wants to crouch beside him, stroke his face and wrap her arms around him. She's also tempted to yank him upright by the shoulders and shake him hard, or slap his face and jolt him back to reality. Grow up, Guildford. Stop snivelling. You're not a frightened boy anymore.

Gulls wheel and cry above the brown sludge tide. If she raises her gaze to the heavens, it seems as if she is flying over the Thames, eastward towards the sea and freedom. Salt hangs heavy in the air even now, a chance to flee, the niggling lure of a dive overboard into the murky depths. Perhaps she could make it to the far bank, treading water amongst the sewage and frothy scum until nightfall. Maybe she could creep ashore amidst the sparse, guttering torches. Slip into the shadows of Southwark's timbered houses or through the narrow twisting warrens of Eastcheap, threading her way past the empty bear-baiting pits and the gong farmers snoring beneath their stinking wagons of nightsoil.

No. That is no way for the baying, foaming mob to remember her. She must not live in their memories as a slithering, decrepit thing, crawling for cover in the hope of a pathetic fugitive life between hovels and haylofts, never more than a careless word from betrayal, capture and public humiliation.

Calm. Certain. Graceful. Dignified. Worthy of any regal queen, though she lost that title long ago.

White stonework looms. The crowd's hollering crescendos. She steadies herself as the barge turns, lurching against the current as they're carried towards the yawning entrance of the Court Gate. Its immense wicket of tar-blackened oak beams awaits them.

What a difference a fortnight makes! She first arrived here a queen on July 10th, resplendent in a heavy green damask gown edged with gold thread, the pale cream sleeves of her kirtle like blooming lilies, flanked by her royal entourage through the Watergate on coronation day. Nine days later, at the stroke of a pen, her royal palace became her prison. The bells of St Paul's pealing over and over again, a riotous jangle of joyful noise across the city, proclaiming Lady Mary the true queen of Albion. And Jane herself just a fool in a paper crown.

Overnight her guards became her gaolers, her royal quarters became her cells; even then her rooms were thinning out; attendants already slipping away, deserting her, her maids slowly vanishing for the safety of their own homes until only three ladies-in-waiting remained by her side. Now, mid-September, she is officially denounced as a usurper, a heretic, a traitor to the crown. An outcast destined for the pyre or the axe. Yet still these three handmaidens remain close behind her, huddled together in the bobbing barge, eyes down and hands clasped as Cranmer murmurs a prayer. Elizabeth Tilney, Mistress Ellen and Mistress Jacob. Heads bowed beneath their demure French hoods, but all three still faithfully united in her shadow.

All her life she has been taught that small things have consequences – the coquettish turn of a head in a dance, the playful glance up through a mask at a ball. So is it now. She must remain steady as the jeering populace gaze their last upon her. The arms of Court Gate swing open, obsequious in their lumbering grace. The Queen's colours already hang high above her from Byward Tower, limp under the baking afternoon sun.

Blank stonework looms overhead, the narrow loup windows and rusty grates overlooking the inner moat like grim-faced sentinels. The stone walls are white in the foetid oppressive heat, embedded flints sparkling like diamonds. She wrinkles her nose at the sickly stench; here the moat has become a sluggish stinking ditch choked with dung and offal from the Tower kitchens. Bobbing filth that even the Thames tides cannot cleanse but merely stir up instead before retreating, leaving behind rotting seaweed and dead decaying fish.

They pass into shade, overshadowed by the looming stone battlements. She shivers at the sudden chill. No human faces peer down from above, just the flap of a raven's wing and its harsh croak overhead. Beyond the vast curtain walls of the Tower she still hears people laughing and cheering, faint cries of derision floating over the ramparts. A seagull swirls overhead, wailing at the deaf stonework. No other sounds but the death-rattle creak of the oarlocks and the sullen ripple of wooden oars easing through the torpid brown slurry.

A pretender-queen, a mistake manhandled onto the throne and then just as quickly pulled off it again. Her father-in-law John Dudley, yes, of course people would remember *him*: Duke of Northumberland, Earl of Warwick, Lord Admiral, the indomitable three-year ruler of England for a sickly boy-King. But Jane? She's just a girl, and before long people would soon forget which girl, exactly: one of the three Grey sisters, someone's sister, someone's second cousin, someone's daughter-in-law.

Nobody important.

She breathes out. But she *was* important, wasn't she? Queen of the realm for over a week, almost two, her ironclad faith unwavering, a pious English rose who'd never wronged a single soul, never a vicious word spat in anger. She will meet her Maker without fear or remorse. This life is just a vale of tears through which all souls must pass.

As if on cue, the Tower cannon booms, startling her, its deep roar rolling out across the murky brown water and echoing off the high crenellated ramparts; she feels the jolt inside, deep in her bones. *They only fire it for persons of note*, she recalls, and feels a warm frisson of gladness shiver through her. Disturbed ravens swirl over St Thomas' Tower like windblown scraps of oily black cloth, their harsh clamour rattling off the walls.

Around the bend, stern-faced guards in crimson velvet line the stone wharf. Their halberds face outwards towards her, axe blades glinting in the sun. The incoming tide laps at the slimy riverside steps. John Brydges, lieutenant of the Tower, awaits them on the Watergate quay; as the boat draws alongside and rocks gently, he bows. 'My lady.'

'Sir John.' She nods back, almost dips a curtsey out of habit before steadying herself. She is still of royal blood. She is of noble birth, not some doleful blushing milkmaid who's pinched the silver spoons.

When the gangplank is run ashore, oars are drawn in and the rowers hold the boat fast to the mooring ropes, the lieutenant offers his hand to her. 'By your leave, my lady.' She takes it and steps up onto dry land once more, light as a feather in her soft-soled velvet shoes.

A glimmer of hope: perhaps she will be

readmitted to her old private chambers where she and her husband lay before her coronation. Not the royal apartments any longer, not now a new queen has laid claim to them. But a pair of empty serviceable rooms for her at least, a cold fireless hearth swept clean of ash and blank lime-washed walls awaiting.

The bleak frown on the lieutenant's face suggests otherwise. Ah, well. More bad news. A faint smile tugs at her lips, a glint of mischief in that freckled face.

'So what now? Am I to be sent to the dungeons, like a common traitor?'

John's eyes crinkle in a wry smile. 'No, madam. You are to remain at the Gentleman Gaoler's house beside my own lodgings. Nathaniel Partridge is a decent fellow and gracious host. Rest assured, you will be treated honourably and allowed visitors, as befits your former title.' He frowns. 'But regrettably, your husband is to be escorted to the Beauchamp Tower for separate confinement. We have our orders.' He inclines his head. 'I remain, Lady Dudley, your most humble servant.'

She glances through the dark archway towards the high keep, looming bleak against the afternoon sun. She is under no illusions; they might treat her with grace and respect, but she still remains a prisoner under lock and key until her grisly fate, in the shadow of the high White Tower. Her husband won't remain in the lieutenant's house anymore, no longer an honoured lord confined under house arrest. Now he will be taken deeper into the Tower, to the inner ward where they keep the traitors, and torture them, too.

She smooths down her black dress, fit for an honourable lady. The queen that once was. Underneath her black brocade lies a hidden petticoat of scarlet velvet, a second armour shielding her heart. Red is the colour of defiance, the colour of life, of love, and martyrdom. And so it is her colour.

She looks back at her companions. Guildford fidgets between the oarsmen, hands twisting in his lap as his brothers mope glumly alongside him. Lords every one of them, yet none man enough to meet her gaze. But Cranmer smiles up at her, rheumy eyes crinkling with fond pride above the grey thicket of his beard. Her three ladies dip their heads. Loyal to a doomed queen. Forever faithful to their short-lived monarch.

We are brave, Your Highness. We won't break and crumble. And neither must you.

She squares her shoulders and climbs the damp slippery steps, calm and resolute. She won't see her eighteenth birthday, but she shall still wear her black embroidered gown and red petticoat until the day she dies – and whenever that day soon dawns, if the poor loveless bastard Mary still huddles on her stolen throne, flinching at every shadow, then at least she will remember Jane. The quiet, gentle English rose who never broke faith. The girl who kept her vows.

HELLCAT

Mary Read is born a disappointment.

When Maggie Read needed more sons, she'd pushed out a daughter instead, flailing and screaming, yet another hungry mouth to feed; a mouth that would require a dowry, later, rather than bring home a welcome bride-price that swells her meagre coffers.

Mary Read has always been a damn difficulty for her mother.

It's the year of our lord 1690. Maggie's sea-faring husband long dead, missing for months now in some faraway sea, two mewling infants who need to be provided for. It's a hard life, blighted by the threat of the unforgiving world. A king whose head is heady with war in Europe, the lurking danger of disease, poverty, withered harvests.

These are times which try men's souls.

It doesn't help that Mary is not exactly a model daughter. It's almost a relief when Mark dies young, snatched away by sickness, and Mary takes his place. Dressed as a boy, enveloped in unfamiliar cloth, clumsy at first in her strange trousers.

She doesn't require much persuading. *Life would be easier*, her mother whispers, *when you're older, you can go to London and be Mary again. Marry, settle down. No one would ever know Mark Read.*

Mary bristles at this. I don't want to settle, she thinks, this is my chance. Mark Read. Rebellion's in her blood.

Opportunities like this are few and far between for farm girls.

Mary Read is dead. Long live Mark Read.

People in the village whisper quietly amongst themselves that "Mark" changed when Mary died; he became harsher, spitting and swearing, causing his poor mother no end of grief. He used to be so sensitive, so quiet, they say, shaking their heads sadly. Something brought out the devil in him.

Fifteen long years later, when the recruiters come, hungry for fresh meat for another of Queen Anne's foreign wars, the villagers all point to Mark Read. There's the scrappy lad you want, they insist. There's a boy made for the fight.

When she sails away to war for the first time she realises that, for once, they were right. Nothing suits her quite as well as battle.

When she's fighting the French for a queen she doesn't care for under a name that isn't even hers, her fellow soldiers question "Mark" on his growing success with women.

. "You can hear 'em moaning from the next house,' one of them whispers. He's a pale boy, fresh out of London. He'll probably die tomorrow, a bullet clipped through his chest, a cannonball wrecking through him like he's freshly churned butter. But tonight they drink and talk. They don't know who they're fighting, not really, nor why, but they know that this is far better than a life of idle vagrancy – many of these men were made for the poorhouses, a lifetime hanging around the whorehouses or worse.

Mary looks at him. He glares back, daring her to disagree. He's probably a virgin, judging by the way his cheeks (that she can see, under all that mud) are tinged pink. *In another life*, she idly wonders, *you could have been my husband*. She tries to imagine those thin hands wrapped around her waist. Then looks down at her own palms blackened by gunpowder, calloused by the sword. Such is her lot in life. She doesn't regret a moment.

'Call it intuition.' She winks. 'The rest's a secret.' She makes a complicated lewd hand gesture, and their surrounding Dutch companions bray with laughter. Coarseness needs no translation. Mary thumps the pale boy on the back, like a brother might, smirking into her beer (or whatever the quartermaster is calling ale these days – it's been a *long* campaign).

She's eighteen and invincible. No one suspects.

One man doesn't laugh. He just watches, lounging by the dying embers in his Dutch blue tunic and red neckerchief, dark eyes glinting in the firelight. Later, in the candlelit back bedroom of a tavern, she'll loosen her hair out of the knotted green ribbon that folds it together, and let her long brown locks tumble down past her shoulders. Later, his eyes won't even widen and his voice will not betray surprise at this fresh revelation. He'll never ask who Mark was, when they lie together amid rumpled sheets.

But that's later. Tonight, they drink.

The next day, the boy dies. It's a paltry ambush, a feeble crackle of muskets from a roadside hedgerow, but his death is short and clean. Far more than many others could hope for, their lives ripped away by the tortuous threads of fate, their last gasps rattling away into burbling gargles of despair. Blood is slashed across her face like a tattoo, it feels like this violence will forever be imprinted on her skin. Sinking deep into her bones.

Many other men die, some English, Scottish, Welsh, Flemish, the French they kill too. Mary doesn't die. She knows what it says in the good book: live by the sword, die by the sword.

And as it just so happens, Mary Read is *very* good with a sword.

Her bunkmate Martin is a fierce fighter and a staunch soldier, but a gentle friend. He listens when she gripes. When she'd vomited for the whole first day of her maiden voyage, he sat close beside her, gently rubbing her back. He shows her a brotherly camaraderie that was softer than most of her crewmates, and she softens to him in turn.

Her mistake.

Martin's neediness grows. He wishes to spirit her away from their dangerous life under arms. He yearns to marry, settle down, start a family. Wants to free her from the chains that bind her to "Mark".

One drunken night in a Dutch tavern later, her world crumbles. Martin spews her secret to their fellow soldiers, slurring about her true gender, their love, their future plans. His plans. He turns away when she pleads her yearning to remain at sea by his side. He scoffs when she pleads to remain at sea by his side. By the time she realizes her narrowing options, it's far too late.

The company know her secret, and they refuse to suffer a woman in their ranks. There's only one path forward: resignation. She and Martin are discharged, marry in the Netherlands and open a family inn near the castle at Breda. But Martin's mother dresses her as "befitting a proper lady" and styles her hair as it grows out longer. Rigid corsets squeeze the air from her lungs, and her bare neck itches as her hair grows longer. Women's shoes are not made for running, and the long rustling skirts are useless for climbing rigging. The calluses on her hands begin to heal over, palms softening with disuse as weeks stretch into months.

The ship lurches beneath her, but she strolls surefooted across the poop deck, adjusting each stride to the roll and sway of the ship. Lets every creak and groan of seasoned timbers tell their secrets from her boots upward.

They're sailing for Jamaica. Mary's not sure what she wants from there, but she knows that there's nothing left for her back in Holland, just hollow memories of better, gentler times. The inn's closed. Her man with dark eyes which had shone in moonlight and firelight (it hurts to remember his name, now, even after) is cold and buried in the

39

ground.

But Martin's death is her deliverance. A childless widow. Free to return to the open sea. Free to cut her hair and wear loose-fitting trousers and roughen her palms on brine-sodden ropes again.

Free to be Mark once more.

She's resurrecting her old disguise, dressed as a man again on this Dutch merchantman. If Mary had anyone to justify it too, she'd probably blag about how dangerous the sea is, the safe anonymity of a man's clothes, her confident demeanour. She can handle herself, but it's better to save the bother of explaining. But Mary doesn't have anyone to justify it too, so she's pulled the loose-fitting britches back on, more familiar than skirts now – she's been Mark longer than she's ever been Mary.

'Sail ahoy!' the lookout calls from the rigging high overhead, pointing west. 'Ship off ta' port!'

Mary hurries up beside the captain on the quarterdeck, takes the spyglass from him and gazes out. She sees the distant black fluttering in the ocean breeze, no more than a league westward. A leering white skull above two crossed swords.

The Jolly Roger. John Rackham's dreaded ensign. Ice shivers up her spine. She's heard enough rumours of "Calico Jack" whispered around tavern firesides. The man's a cold-blooded, merciless monster, even in those laughable striped patchwork trousers of his.

She lowers the spyglass and frowns down at the crew gathering on the main deck below, bristling with what meagre weapons they can scrounge. For some unknown, godforsaken reason, they've decided that they should try and fight their way out of it – a feeble attempt, she supposes, to delay the inevitable butchery ahead.

Probably something to do with insurance. It all boils down to money somewhere.

Her choice becomes immediately obvious, before the first cannon blast: fight with this crew, die alongside them. Or, she thinks, memories of the bloody battlefields of Europe, laughing around the campfire, somewhere she's not a disappointment but a brutal and magnificent success.

These pirates want a fight? They'll bloody well get one.

Smoke billows from the oncoming sloop. A second later, the dull crump of cannonfire. A tearing, howling shriek. Chainshot and canister. Mary feels the ship shudder as the heavy iron balls smash deep into her bows. A lethal blizzard of iron scythes the length of the main deck, shredding wood and flesh alike.

Wretched whimpers echo behind her. The

captain has crumpled to his knees beside the wheel, ashen-faced and frozen with bowel-loosening terror.

Mary rolls her eyes. He'll be no use at all.

The merchant vessel is fogged with smoke and confusion, a mess of splintered wood and shredded sail. The ship draws alongside its crippled prey, jeering pirates crowding the rigging as they wave cutlasses and boarding axes. The first grappling hook whirls overhead. The pirates swarm aboard, roaring for blood.

Mary makes her choice.

The crew of the *Vanity* overrun the merchant ship, cleaving and hacking down all before them. Yelling with bloodlust, they storm up the broad splintered stairs onto the quarterdeck.

And stumble to a halt. The roars die on sun-cracked lips.

A man with a jagged scar down his face holds a pistol to the head of the captain, strong and still. The cutlass in his other hand drips with blood, pressing into the neck of another sailor. This isn't just a turncoat's last-minute betrayal; three of *Vanity*'s crew lie sprawled across the quarterdeck, crusty salt-bitten veterans of a dozen bloody battles now stiff and twisted in death. The marauders shift uneasily, gawping at this unexpected standoff.

'Cap'n Rackham?' the armed man calls out, pressing the muzzle of his pistol harder into the captain's quivering head. 'You good to parley?' The captain flinches forward, the white scrap of surrender shaking in his hand.

A blond man and red-haired woman elbow their way through the hushed crowd. The redhead's eyes slide over the frozen scene, and her lip curls.

'Me name's Anne,' she drawls in a thick Irish twang, then rolls a shoulder to the man lurking behind her. 'This here's Jack.'

They don't need further introduction. There aren't any other pairs in the Caribbean like them – they're infamous and inseparable; Bonny and Rackham. Anne's fearsome reputation precedes her. A woman aboard ship, respected by her peers and feared by her enemies. Her twin cutlasses hang heavy on both hips, a weapon slid into every crevice of her body, wrapped between layers of dark cloth, broad hat obscuring most of her freckled face from the unrelenting scorch of sun. Rackham contrasts Anne; his yellowing shirt hangs open in the light breeze, a long jacket that conceals nothing, his sabre dangling almost delicately from his cocked hip, his suntanned chest bared to the elements.

The armed man gazes coolly back at them, considering. He's handsome yet his pores ooze violence; scarred, tall, dark hair knotted round a bandana the same deep crimson of a fresh gaping wound. The blood-slicked blade presses harder into his captive's neck, earning a whimper. His appraising eyes slide from Jack to Anne.

'I've heard of you both,' he says, with a lilting inflection Anne isn't familiar with: somewhere from the continent, not French. Perhaps Holland, judging from how the *u*'s roll off his tongue. There have been enough wars on the mainland to create a generation of listless men with battle singing in their blood, who find their calling in the freedom of the high seas.

'The name's Read,' the man continues, his smouldering gaze sliding over Anne. 'Mark Read. You lookin' for new volunteers?'

Anne shivers. Not from the cold.

They're celebrating. Nassau has been won back (for now, the niggling voice in Jack's head whispers, he's already won and lost this town before – not again, he swore, never again), and even that dour-faced killjoy Captain Flint can see the attraction in letting loose for one night. It might be a piss-up, but it's well deserved.

A drink is pressed into Jack's hands, different from the usual tavern swill – the bottle looks Spanish, expensive. The owner is the newest addition to their crew, the deadly one with the scarlet bandana who faced down an entire crew without flinching, three men dead at his feet.

'Thought you deserved somethin' good,' Read grunts. He's bearing a few more marks than last time they talked, including a cutlass slice down the collarbone, a knotted white scar which disappears under his grimy shirt. 'My treat.'

Jack raises an eyebrow. No one in Nassau is known for giving gifts freely. This will be an interesting dance. 'Cheers, shipmate.' He nods his thanks, watching Read's reaction. He's impassive, but almost a twitch of humour in his mouth. As Anne wanders over to join them, Jack wonders what kind of dance they've started.

Jack's cabin tilts and sways around them, awash with flickering candlelight. From outside echoes the bawdy singing of their crewmates, the creaking groan of brine-soaked timbers, the distant toll of the harbour bell.

'You're a damn good fighter,' Read tells Anne, taking a swig of his own bottle of Tequila. 'A good thinker, too,' he adds. Jack watches Mark as he drinks, short dark hair tucked under a crimson bandana, more red cloth wrapped thickly around his throat. Read's a handsome man (Jack doesn't touch, not these days, but that doesn't mean he can't look, can't appreciate when the mood strikes him), all sharp lines and a battle-hardened body hidden beneath salt-cracked leather. He talks sparingly, voice husky, only when he needs to. He reminds Jack of Anne, funnily enough. He sees the lines of Read's face, the smooth unblemished skin with no hint of stubble, and speculates.

'You work well together,' Read finishes.

Anne – hatless for once, her fiery red curls shining in the candlelight – blushes, reaches forward and plucks the bottle out of Read's hands. 'We're a team,' she purrs, ''til the end of it.' Calico Jack (a new moniker, but all good – all infamous – pirates need a nickname, standing around the likes of Long John Silver and Blackbeard, always a flair for melodrama) and Anne Bonny, until they're cold and rotting in the ground. It's a deal he's happy with.

'My captain –' Read stops, corrects himself. 'In the army. Before. My captain always said I was pragmatic.' He reaches back for the Tequila from Anne, but his hand lingers on her bare wrist momentarily, a single finger brushing her sun-bronzed skin. Almost a gentle caress.

46

Jack continues to wonder.

Read takes a swig, mouth twisted in amusement. 'I had to ask him what that meant. Realistic, he said it was. Sensible.' He pauses again, considering. Then: 'I had a man, once.'

Jack and Anne smile. Neither of them are surprised by this revelation, to be honest. It's a big wide world to explore out there, all kinds of hidden treasures awaiting. Who are they to judge another crewmate's desires? Mark's lethal with a sword and has a razor-sharp mind for tactics and seamanship, that's all that matters out in the deep.

Read taps his bottle, lost in fond recollection. 'He was a soldier, I met him in Holland.' The soft tenderness in his voice is plain, then. 'Bought an inn together. The Three Horseshoes. Wasn't much, but …' He sighs. 'He was kind. I loved him.'

Anne rescues a fresh bottle from the floor, uncorks and raises it in a toast. 'To lost loves.'

They all clink bottles and knock back a slug. It's damn fine Tequila. Read smacks his lips, then grins at them both. 'I know a good bet when I see one. You two, you're a good bet.'

Jack raises his eyebrows, and can't quite smother the flush of warm pride which slices through him.

Anne raises her bottle of Tequila. 'To good bets.'

Jack grins at them both. 'Drink up, me hearties,

yo ho,' he sing-songs raggedly. Then his head lolls back, the half-empty bottle slips from his twitching fingers, and he begins to snore.

Read rises from his stool, squeezing Anne's shoulder. He winks down at her. 'I reckon there's a fresh bottle downstairs with our names on it. Fancy helping me look?'

Smiling, Anne lets herself be pulled away.

They're pressed back in the corner of the darkened storeroom. Read's lips are ghosting a trail of fire across Anne's jawline, her throat, the soft hollow of her clavicle, down the flushed swell of her bosom. Anne's hands are roaming everywhere, clutching desperately at Read's hips, his collar, his shoulders, pawing at his belt. His soft lips swallow her needy moan; he tastes of rum, cloves and seaspray. She hooks a leg over his thigh and grinds against him, her body thrumming with desire. Her harsh urgent panting echoes loud in the gloom, she needs pressure and friction and sweet *release* ...

There's suddenly far too many layers of clothing between them and far too many buckles.

'Clothes,' Anne rasps breathlessly between heated kisses. 'Off. Now.'

Read fumbles clumsily with his jacket. 'I'm tryin', love, I just ... bugger!' He snorts a laugh as

Anne melts against him, giggling. Then she stifles a moan as Read's free hand drifts lower, slips inside her britches, her drawers, begins to stroke.

'I want,' she pants as she arches into Read, grinding down, aching for more. 'I want.'

'And I'll give,' Read tells her, resting their foreheads together. 'Whatever you want, love. I'll give.' His words drag across her skin, his voice husky with lust, making her shudder.

Someday, the doubter in her warns, *all this will end. Jack will discover this deception. The crew will disown you. Read will leave you. You are not worthy. There will be another, a proper lady deserving of his love. He will find another woman, a better woman.*

But I will be first, she snarls back at herself, nails biting into Read's back, throat bared for his lips as his fingers curl deep inside her. *I was first to have his love, and I will be last to lose it.*

She drops to her knees, untucks Read's shirt and glides her palms over the smooth, hard planes of his toned torso. She can't help but rake her fingernails across her lover's stomach, digging in. Marking him. Claiming him. She hears Read gasp above her and her smile deepens into a greedy smirk of triumph.

'Wait,' Read whispers, placing his hands over

Anne's to halt their frantic desperation.

She frowns. 'What? Too much?'

'No, it's not that.' He gently pulls her up, holding her out at arm's length.

Dismay shudders through her, drenching her insides with ice even as she feels herself nodding. 'You're right. Too soon. We don't have to –'

But Read just presses a finger to her lips and smiles before stepping back past the stacked barrels of salt pork. Anne's body screams with aching dread. She's failed. She's spoiled everything, blundering in like a love-stricken fool. Read will turn away and walk back upstairs, and that will be the end of it.

Except …

He stands there in the dank, stinking gloom, swaying with the gentle swell of the ship, a sliver of moonlight slicing across his smiling face. Silence between them; nothing but the creaking ribs of their ship and the faint tinkle of rum bottles jostling in a half-empty crate.

'I've been living a lie,' Read murmurs. 'I'm sorry, Anne.'

He reaches up and slowly pulls off his red bandana, then shakes his hair free. Dark curls, longer than Anne supposed, tumble down in a tangled wave across his face. Read loosens his neckerchief and pulls it away; scarlet cloth slides free revealing the pale smooth line of Read's throat – without the telltale bob of an Adam's apple.

He hesitates, then begins unbuttoning his shirt. Then, holding Anne's hungry gaze, he opens it. Baring his secret.

Two perfect pale islets, their honey-gold swell under the lamplight.

A handsome man becomes a handsome woman.

Anne breathes out.

Read blushes. 'I should reintroduce myself, I suppose.' She swallows. 'My name's Read. Mary Read.'

Anne's eyes gleam in the moonlight. She takes Read's hand and lifts it to her lips, tenderly kissing the callused knuckles.

'It's my pleasure, Mary,' she purrs, and the night ahead is full of possibilities.

They couldn't be more different. Anne is the comely tavern beauty who draws men's eyes; all sun-kissed freckles, tempting curves beneath her blouse and skirts and a wild fiery red mane that tumbles down past her shoulders. Mary is flat chested and straight hipped with high stern cheekbones, a broad nose and an impish smile. She dresses like a man too, with billowing waistcoat and loose-fitting britches that mask the sway of her hips, her crow-black curly hair cropped short around her ears, easily knotted back into a man's ponytail.

But they both know a woman's pleasure inside out. How to tease it out and savour it like a rich fine wine, in endless rolling waves of blissful ecstasy with fingers, tongue and teeth. A gentle frenzy of stroking hands and gasping breaths and grinding hips, bathed in soft candlelight amid sweat-dampened sheets. And for this forbidden love Mary knows she'll burn in the fires of Hell.

Of all the sins she's committed, from blasphemy to adultery, to piracy and cold-blooded murder, all could and would be forgiven on the Day of Judgement. All except the abomination against the flesh. To taste Anne in those secret depths is to taste of Satan. She knows that.

But Hell be damned. Life is for living. Life is for the here and now, not the Hereafter.

'Wow,' Anne sighs to the cabin ceiling, her head slumping back into rumpled pillows. 'That was … *wow.*'

'You too,' Mary whispers between her naked thighs. Soft and reverent like a prayer, a benediction, a victory without price. Anne's hands tighten in her hair, fingers twisting with eagerness.

The stuttering sounds tumbling from her mouth are raw and gasping, a kind of pleading she didn't know she could ever do.

When Anne finally looks down – chest heaving and glassy-eyed – Mary is gazing up at her, eyes alight with wonder and a coy smirk dancing at her mouth, licking Anne's glistening nectar from her lips, and dear *God* but that's downright obscene.

'Christ alive, Mary,' Anne sighs.

Mary's eyes twinkle. 'Again?' she asks, grinning. The husky murmur of her voice is a warm caress of infinite gentleness, and Anne feels as venerated as a goddess before her.

'Yes. Dear God, *yes.*'

Anne's body clenches with desire as Mary crawls up her body, peppering tiny chaste kisses here and lazy, languid kisses there.

'C'mere,' she groans and straddles Anne, before pulling her into a searing kiss.

Finally they break apart, gasping for air, foreheads nestled against each other. Mary is gazing down, her eyes glittering with adoration.

It takes Anne a few wild heartbeats to catch her breath again. 'What?' she hears herself quietly ask.

A smile tugs at Mary's lips. 'Just wonderin' how someone like me got so lucky, that's all.'

Her cheeks flush and she drops her gaze. She

doesn't say anything more, but Anne hears it all the same: the doubt and uncertainty, the 'my happiness is only temporary' and the 'I still think you deserve better'. They're still there, hiding and latching onto the space between Mary's words, like ghosts of old friends coming to claim their due.

Anne won't let them win.

She vows to herself there and then: they will never win.

Her hand drifts up to cup Mary's flushed cheek, thumb gently stroking in a soothing motion. Her heart clenches with warm tenderness as Mary sighs and leans into her touch, eyes fluttering shut.

'You and me both, darling,' Anne whispers.

Mary blinks back another swell of fresh tears; it's this bed, and who they become inside of it. Outside, they are a faithful first mate and a loyal sailor, drenched in responsibilities and outward appearances, their defences always up amid the other deckhands. But here, in this blessed no man's land of soft sheets and golden candlelight, they are human, vulnerable, bared to each other.

They are each other's secret, for now and always.

Heavy boots on the stairs outside. Clomping unsteadily towards them. Mary's head jerks upright, staring at the door. 'Aw, hell,' she curses.

Anne lurches upright, fumbling for the bedsheets. 'Quick! Get behind the –'

BANG. The cabin door bursts open.

Jack Rackham stands frozen in the doorway, rum bottle in hand. His bloodshot eyes slide over the scene: Anne lying creamily naked amid tangled sheets, the still-clothed figure straddling her hips, wide dark eyes staring back at him. Claiming his wife. His confidante. In his bed. Their private bed!

The bottle clatters to the floor. Jack's eyes bulge with outrage. 'Read!' he bellows and surges forward, clawing at his cutlass.

Until Mary twists around and rips her shirt aside. Baring herself to him.

Jack stumbles to a stupefied halt, gulping like a stranded fish in dumbfounded silence. Mary glares defiantly back at him, bare-breasted and utterly unashamed.

Anne's never seen anyone quite so beautiful.

The only sound is the faint rattle of buttons pattering onto the floor.

'You – you're a woman?' Jack finally rasps, still gawping.

'Aye,' Mary declares icily. 'Y'see? No threat. I ain't hiding anymore.'

'Aaagggh.' Jack gropes blindly for a chair and slumps into it. 'Well … fuck me sideways,' he murmurs, awestruck.

Mary feels a warm wave of smartness wash over her, like gentle summer rain kissing her skin.

'Wait your turn, Cap'n,' she snarks, and beneath her Anne cackles into the pillows.

Of course Jack keeps their secret, and from thenceforth shares his bed with the pair of them. Fair trade, all in all. None of the other twelve crewmates know of Read's true identity. Not a humble sort, though, that Calico Jack. How he struts about the quarterdeck like a puffed-up popinjay the next day! Like a braggart who's seized the richest treasure haul in the whole Spanish Main.

Anne rolls her eyes whenever he swaggers past with a knowing wink; amid the dank squalor of Nassau's reeking taverns, he'd first stood out from the motley rabble of leering buccaneers like a parrot among pigeons. A rare gallant among vagabonds, scallywags, marauders and bloodthirsty cutthroats. A gold sovereign in shit.

Still, she's almost tempted to frogmarch his arse to the stern railing and pitch him overboard.

Almost.

They're a lazy tangle of limbs, warm and cosy and deliciously naked. Beside her Anne feels Mary stirring from the warm drowsy depths of slumber. Mary rises and yawns, her lean muscles rippling in the faint dawn light.

Anne's insides clench; Mary's back is etched with her violent past, her lithe creamy skin crisscrossed with crooked battle scars, a scattered patchwork of slices and bullet wounds. Her ugly history of warfare stretches shoulder to shoulder, spanning across continents of taut muscle. Mary scoops a discarded shirt off the floor, pulls it on and saunters over to the chair by the aft window, gazing out across the bay.

Anne sure appreciates the view.

Behind her, Jack snores like the Devil. Anne bites back a fond grin; it's both irritating and endearing.

The *William* rocks beneath them, faintly creaking and groaning with each new swell. Their second ship together, a twelve-ton English sloop commandeered with guile and guts, serenaded by the murmuring waves. The open ocean has been a gentle comforting lullaby to Anne for many months now: as familiar now as the wailing echo of gullsong, twin cutlasses heavy on her hips and a broad-brimmed hat low on her brow. It's a scrappy ship but fast, a good prize hunter. They'll mould her into something fierce, something to inspire fear and awe, under the grinning skull and crossed swords.

Rackham and Bonny – and Read, she knows now, watching the wind ruffle Mary's dark hair. She's as much a part of this as they both are. Her secret sits safely in this cabin under unspoken trust, its importance reverberating between the three of them.

Anne watches the dawn light lick Mary's bare skin, who looks like she's savouring this peaceful moment; all her layers of disguise and pretence stripped away under the warm kiss of the morning sun.

Anne slides over Jack's form sprawled across the bed, before rising with a fond smile. She crosses the room to lean against the window beside Mary, not bothering to dress. The warmth of the sun slides over her, bathing her skin in gold. She preens as Mary's hungry eyes rake up and down her, biting her lip. Anne basks in her silent adoration.

'This is the beginning of something, isn't it?' Mary asks, reaching out her hand to Anne.

Anne reaches back.

The setting sun is fast dipping towards the horizon, turning the sea into glittering mercury and the sky into pale blue crystal tinged with rose pink streaks.

William is moored just off Dry Harbour Bay in a sheltered inlet. Safely hidden from prying eyes. Only a hundred feet or so from the sandy cove. Close enough for Anne to see the breeze gently rustle the palm trees. A shrill whine buzzes past her ear, and she swats away a curious midge. This coastline is a four-mile stretch of sand and swamp, a hotbed for mosquitoes.

'Isn't it beautiful?' Mary sighs, turning to her beloved with the whole brilliance of the setting sun reflected in her dark eyes. 'So still.'

'A little *too* still if you ask me,' Anne mutters, gaze flitting to the distant horizon.

'Anne,' Mary groans, slow and deliberate like she's nursing a headache. 'Stop being such a wet blanket.'

But Anne continues nervously scanning the waves for any sign of trouble. 'What if someone spots us here?'

Mary plucks the spyglass out of Anne's hand. 'Quit that nonsense right now and kiss me,' she purrs.

Anne rolls her eyes and pulls her close, fists clenched in her collar. Mary's hands slide lower, tightening possessively over Anne's hips. A quick sideways glance to check they're still alone on deck.

They are.

The rest of the crew have been drinking since noon, and by the muffled sound of crazed drunken laughter and snatches of smutty verses below, they have no intention of stopping anytime soon. Safe enough. They share a long lingering kiss, each intoxicated on the other's rum-sweetened breath.

Anne pulls away first, dropping her gaze with a sigh. Mary frowns as Anne's deep green eyes cloud with worry. She tenderly cups her chin. 'What ails you, love?'

Anne huffs a breath. 'I can't tell. Just a feelin', is all.' She steps away to the quarterdeck railing, fidgeting with the spyglass. By now, the great golden orb of sun has melted into the sea and the darkening sky is streaked with fire.

Anne's eyes widen. 'There!' She raises the spyglass again. 'I told you so. Right there on the horizon, look! White sails. Westwards.'

'Lemme see.' Mary pulls the spyglass from Anne's hand and clambers up the rigging for a better view, shimmying from rope to rope.

'Aye,' she calls down, 'It's another ship, for sure.'

Anne shades her eyes and squints. 'What flag?'

'I can't see yet, you daft fool.'

'Well, it sure as hell sees us,' Anne mutters, 'and

it's heading straight for us like it means business.'

There's a certain stretch of uncertain limbo, between the first sighting of a distant ship and the learning of its true nature and intent, where fate hangs in the balance. The world holds its breath.

To spy a far-off sail at sea is to stand upon a threshold. A teetering knife edge. A gateway to the unknown. It could be fellow Brethren of the Coast come to swell their ranks like the nine additional English mariners drinking below. Or a defenceless merchant vessel ripe for plunder. Until it got close enough to read its fluttering ensign, it could be anything.

This could be *the* ship. The one that holds the grand prize. Or it could be the other one. The ship of despair. Of reckoning. The one that's been a long time coming. The ship that spells their certain doom.

Mary is high overhead, gazing out. 'It's a sloop, all right. Big one. It's … oh *shit*.'

'What is it?'

'Get the lads!' Mary screams, tumbling down the rigging into her arms, frantic with dread.

'*What*, Mary? What is it?'

'British!'

Ice slithers down Anne's spine, sinking its claws deep as she stares out in speechless terror.

A Royal Navy sloop of that kind, and in these waters could mean only one thing.

'Pirate hunters,' she curses.

The fatal pin of reckoning that punctures their bubble of bliss, as the scene aboard ship erupts into chaos. Anne dashes across the main deck to the cargo hold, peering down into the reeking gloom below.

'Jack!' she bellows. 'Get yer arse up here now! We got trouble!'

Glass tinkles. A drunken giggle. Eventually Jack saunters up on deck with a cocksure swagger, followed by his two favourite lackeys. Jack's face is pallid and yellow, his hat on sideways; a dandyish affectation brought about by the excessive consumption of rum punch. He's still stubbornly clutching a lime as if he'd much rather be below deck, his glazed eyes two poached eggs wobbling in a bowl of fish chowder – proof he's been going ten rounds with the bottle and steadily losing.

'What'n the devil'ssh name's a matter wid yew?' he slurs, swaying with drink.

'See for yourself!' cries Anne, thrusting the spyglass in his hand. Jack nonchalantly tosses aside the lime he's carrying and straightens his hat. He raises the spyglass shakily to his eye, peers for a long moment. A vein throbs in his temple.

'Bollocks!'

Jack Rackham never was the best pirate in the world. Far from it. A far better drinker than a fighter, he isn't the bravest or the brightest either. Not even the most handsome (that would be Mary) but he's still *hands down* the best dressed pirate that had ever lived, finely draped in dyed East Indian calico cloth, flaunting his brazen fashion sense. But you can't get by on appearances alone in this blood-soaked line of work, and Anne hopes against hope that Jack's made of tougher mettle than she fears. The crew dither on the quarterdeck, gazing nervously at the approaching vessel.

'Orders, Cap'n?' one asks, fingers drumming on his cutlass hilt.

'Lower the mainsail,' Jack orders, rubbing his eyes and trying to shake the fog from his aching skull. 'Ready the topgallants, nice an' easy like. Don't give 'em any reason to jitter. And prime that swivel gun. Wait 'til I give the signal, then cut anchor.'

Mary whirls on him. 'We'll never outrun 'em!'

'We don't *need* to outrun 'em, Read,' Jack snarls, 'just need to give 'em the slip. We'll lose 'em over by that there reef.'

Night is beginning to close about them as the other ship draws alongside. A hulking Sloop of

War, with twelve enemy guns and bristling with Royal Marines. There must be forty of them at least, all lined up on deck, bayoneted muskets at the ready, implacable sentinels silhouetted against the last glow of sunset.

'Identify yourselves!' comes the cry from the Navy ship.

'Ahoy there!' Jack cries jovially. 'We're fellow countrymen! What gives?'

'Your name?'

'You first, mate.'

'Captain Jonathan Barnet of the *Albion*, from Jamaica.'

'Ahoy Cap'n, what can I do for ye?'

The grim-faced Englishman raises a scrap of parchment. 'I have here a Letter of Marque signed by Governor Sir Nicholas Lawes. Therein is a list of names of all those suspected of being, or of harbouring, pirates. These are to be brought to await justice at Port Royal, by order of His Majesty King George.'

Another English monarch? Mary wonders. Bloody hell, they *do* run out fast.

Barnet lowers the letter. 'And so I say again … *your name, sir?*'

'Lie!' Anne hisses in Jack's ear. 'Say anything. We're just humble merchants heading for Montego

64

Bay!'

But Jack's face darkens. A maddened gleam flickers deep in his eyes. A self-confident smirk that Anne has seen far too many times before. Whether from drink or pride, she doesn't know, but he puffs out his chest and boldly declares, 'My name is Jack Rackham, of Cuba.'

Jonathan's eyes harden to flints. He signals to his men. 'Strike to British colours and stand by to be boarded!'

Rackham barks a scornful laugh. 'We'll strike no strikes!' He lets loose the swivel gun; Barnet dives for cover as the deck rail explodes into jagged splinters.

'Sever the anchor!' Jack yells through thick clouds of smoke, but it's too late. The naval sloop's gunports erupt in a full return broadside; cannons roar and the mainmast's boom spar cracks onto the deck. Split asunder. Completely severed.

They're trapped.

A crackling hail of musket fire rakes the crippled ship. Shouts. Screams. Moans.

Mary bares her teeth as the first grappling hooks clatter across the deck. In seconds they'll be swarmed by twoscore pig-faced grunts of Empire.

'Come get it, you cunts!' Anne bellows, firing her flintlock into the void as Mary draws her razor-edged cutlass. She's handy with a blade and will surely dispatch a redcoat or two before they meet their bitter end.

But something's wrong.

As the smoke finally clears, Anne and Mary see they are all alone on the blood-stained deck. The crewmen, seeing the hopelessness of their peril, have scuttled below to the safe solace of their bottles. Blasted cowards!

Mary's blood boils. 'Come on, you lily-livered pox-ridden bastards!' she snarls at the darkness. 'If there's still any man among you, come up an' fight like men!'

No answer. Enraged, Mary fires her pistol down into the hold. A muffled cry. The heavy thump of a body.

Anne seizes her arm and heaves her back, restraining her struggling lover. 'Mary! No time! The game's up!' She stands back to back with Mary, chest heaving as her bared cutlasses gleam in the moonlight. Eager for blood.

Mary breathes out, her heart singing with joy. Their ship is doomed, their fates sealed. Her whimpering crewmates cower in the hold. Only one grisly end awaits them all, to dance their last jig at the end of a rope. But when this pack of snivelling puppies is led away to the gallows, she will be the one to stand tall, to show the world what it means to be free, wild and strong. She and Anne both.

The first redcoats swing aboard.

Both women roar back.

Barnet struts across the gangplank onto the crippled *William*, lip curling at the scene before him: two bound women on their knees side by side, arms lashed tightly with rope. Surrounded by a ring of cruel bayonets they both glare back, bloodied and battered. Barnet forces down a surge of grudging admiration; it took six Marines each to overwhelm and bludgeon them into the deck with boots, sword hilts and musket butts. But the ship is his.

Not without cost. *William*'s deck is littered with dead redcoats, seven Marines in all sprawled out, slumped against the mast or draped over the railing.

'You down below!' he calls to the shadowy figures huddled in the gloomy hold. 'Come up! You're prisoners of the crown now!'

A chorus of dispirited groans, then a weak quavering voice answers: 'W–we surrender!'

'You do? Jolly good.' Barnet paces across the deck to the kneeling women, face twisted in contempt. 'Well, well,' he drawls. Miss Bonny. Calico Jack's first mate. I've just been *dying* to meet you.'

Anne smirks back through bloodied teeth. 'Pleasure's all mine, Captain. I'd shake yer hand, but, well ...' she nods down at her bonds, '... I'm a little *tied up* at the moment.'

Barnet's smile fades as he gazes over the other captive. 'And who's this fascinating lady?'

Mary glowers up through a black eye, blood trickling from a gash on her temple. 'Name's Read,' she spits, 'and I ain't no lady!'

Barnet's eyes glitter. 'I can see that.' He paces before them, gloating. 'You're part of a dying breed. The world's ever shrinking, no more secret havens anymore. Nowhere to hide. A new era's dawning, one without you pirate scum.' He waves an arm over the endless rolling ocean. 'We rule the waves now. Can't you see? Or are you destined to run and hide like rats until Judgement Day and the trumpets sound? Hm?'

Mary raises her bloody head in a proud, defiant grin. 'Or you could surrender.'

Anne snorts, reaches across and squeezes her hand.

Barnet's face hardens, eyes bulging. 'Men!' he barks, and the Marines stiffen to attention. 'Clap them in irons and take them aboard for Spanish Town; may they *rot in Hell!*'

Mary uncurls on the filthy floor. Manacles clink on her wrists. A sigh rattles out of her. Her eyes flutter open.

The stone floor is cold and hard beneath her, and her cell reeks of stale piss. The nausea almost makes her gag. Better lie completely still or else she'll throw up. Is it morning yet? How long has she even been here? Days? Weeks?

In the vivid darkness that swims before her, visions flicker with the distant crashing of waves, floating through her throbbing mind.

She stands in the bows watching the grey Atlantic roll beneath them, listening to the gulls scream as Nassau recedes behind her with every wave. The familiar creak and slap of the sails.

Her palms hover at her hips, brushing the smooth walnut grips of her twin flintlock pistols. Shined clean just this morning, barrels swabbed and freshly greased. Primed, loaded and ready for anything. Mary rocks with the sway of the ship, blinking seaspray from her eyes. Under the blistering noonday sun and not a second glance from her crewmates. Not a single man leering and spitting at a woman in trousers standing alone on the foredeck. Clad as a trueborn fighter with billowing jacket, long trousers loose like sails at full wind and a bandana wrapped tight around her head.

A plague had driven her west – a hot wind, a stunted harvest of blighted fields, her mother's lashing tongue, the scorn of her brothers in arms, the whimper of her yearning heart, a way out, the whisper of the open sea. Calling her home.

She's right where she belongs, savouring the next sighting of distant prey and the stench of gunpowder smoke drifting on the salt breeze. The wind would fill the sails with a snap as loud as cannon fire as they prepared to board the next merchant ship and take whatever they wished – jewels or gold or burning kisses with *William*'s first mate. Cannon rolls as thunder and cutlass crackled as lightning –

An iron door clangs shut. Mary is wrenched from her daydreams back into the stinking present.

Shafts of sunlight slice through the bars high above. A breeze threads into the room, stirring the stale air inside it, carrying the jumbled scents of outside: dust from the dry street; a hint of a pie baking somewhere close by, the acrid sweetness of caramelising apple; the sour reek of dogshit. Sunlight ripples on her skin. Every now and again the faint voices of passersby catapult odd words into her cell, severed from sense, small bubbles of sound seeping into the cloying silence. Overlaid over everything is the joyful hubbub of Port Royal's bustling harbour. The creak of timbers. The cries of sailors and seagulls. The distant rumble of the sea itself, ever present, ever soothing. The sounds of freedom.

But here they are drowned out by the stifling echoes of prison. The nearby scrape of a heavy iron door. The rustling shuffle of manacled prisoners, chains clinking on their wrists and ankles. A distant moan of despair. In the corridor outside she can hear the efficient, deathly clip of the guards' steel-tipped boots.

Her mind drifts further back, to the green hills and valleys of her childhood. The effigy of a previous life swims before her: gently rolling fields dappled with sheep and the sweet aftertaste of Rose Wilkin's strawberry jam. She has not spared thought for Plymouth in a very long time. Why now?

Now she is elsewhere, walking through a landscape she doesn't recognise. It is cool here, and quiet. She is all alone. Snow is falling, softly, endlessly, on and on. It piles up on the woodland path around her, shrouding fallen leaves and hedgerows, carpeting broad fields; it weighs down tree branches; it transforms everything into whiteness, blankness, quilted stillness. The silence clamps down. The blessed coolness, the glittering silver light is soothing. She wants only to lie down amid this thick endless blanket of new-fallen snow, to rest herself awhile; her legs are numb, her arms ache, her head is pounding. To lie down, to surrender herself, to stretch out in this glistening, thick white blanket: what relief it would bring her. Something is whispering that she must not lie down, she cannot give in to this desire. Whatever could it be? She's fought long and hard all her life. Why shouldn't she rest?

She lowers herself to the thick white carpet of snow, placing both palms onto the crisp, crystalline skin, watching her hands sink into blessed coolness. How welcoming it all feels! How comforting! How right! Not too cold, not too hard. She lies down, shoulder crunching into snow, pressing her cheek to the softness. The glaring whiteness of it makes her squint, so she closes her eyes, just for a moment, just enough to rest and gather her strength once more. She isn't dropping off to sleep, she *isn't*. She mustn't. She will carry on. She isn't finished yet. But she needs to rest, just for a moment. She opens her eyes, reassuring herself the world still lies around her, shrouded in soft soothing white, and then lets her eyes drift shut. Just for now. Calm. Quiet. Peaceful …

'Mary?'

Awake. She's awake now. She's up. Her eyes are open, she's awake. What the hell.

'Is … is that you?' the voice croaks, as dry as ash. Mary squints through the gloom, and her breath hitches; Anne is slumped against the bars of her neighbouring cell, breathing hoarsely.

Gritting her teeth, Mary drags herself across the filthy flagstones, damp wisps of straw clinging to her elbows as she crawls over. Her stomach muscles groan with agony. She sags bone-weary against the metal bars, struggling to sit upright as her forehead presses into cold hard iron. She swallows, fingers groping through the bars until they brush soft skin. 'H-hey, Anne.'

'Hi,' Anne mumbles back. 'Together again, love?'

Mary huffs a ragged laugh. 'Wouldn't miss it.'

'How're we doin'?'

'Same as always.'

'That bad, huh?'

'Mm.' Mary forces a weary smile. 'Seems our luck's finally run out, eh?' The rusty chuckle tumbles out of her, dissolving into a fresh wave of coughing that claws her throat raw.

Anne's eyes cloud with concern. She worms an arm through the bars and touches Mary's forehead, then flinches back with a curse. 'Damn it, Mary, you're burning up.'

Is she? Is that what this surge of nauseating heat is? Her face aches, as if her bones lie open to the foetid heat. She hears Anne crawl away, the rattle of an iron bucket. Water dripping. Then Anne's gentle voice, closer now: 'Here.' Blessed coolness strokes across her brow. She closes her eyes as Anne swabs the grime from her cheeks, wiping away her unfallen tears with the damp rag.

That's what brought her low? *That's* what defeated her? Not a crippling battle wound, not vicious shrapnel from a cannon blast, not a lucky sword thrust. Just a damn creeping fever that she can't shake? She bares her teeth and tries to force it down, but it is too great, too strong, too vicious. An enemy far too powerful to resist, even for her. It has wreathed and tightened its slimy tendrils around her, sunk its claws deep, and is refusing to surrender its clammy grip. It smells musky, dank and salty. It has crept up on her, cornered her here in this squalid hellhole of rotting wetness where she stews in sweat, in her soiled underclothes.

'It's all my fault …'

Anne frowns. 'Eh?'

'I brought you here.' Guilt uncurls inside her, gnawing at her ribs. 'You didn't deserve all this, I

74

should've saved you, maybe I could've –'

'Horseshit, Mary,' Anne cuts her off. 'We've been together every day since we first met. I *know* you.' She taps a finger under her bruised right eye. 'I've seen more shit than you can even dream of, lass. I've done plenty godawful things with Jack, and you think *you're* the bad egg? I see you hide those tears when you think I can't tell.' She presses her face close to the bars. 'We're pirates, love. Comes with this life we chose. P'raps we'll die tomorrow. P'raps not. But we'll face it together. Just like always.' She snorts. 'So quit lying to yourself, Mary, 'cause you can't lie for *shit*.'

Mary huffs a laugh, then sighs as Anne tenderly strokes her forehead. The hushed silence stretches, then:

'What was it Jack used to say?' Anne asks.

Mary gazes into empty space, brow furrowed. A sweltering autumn day, the streets of Port Royal crammed with jeering townsfolk spitting venom, the hangman's cart clattering through the prison gates. Rackham glaring back alongside his four fellow condemned, before the creak of the trapdoor and the final awful crack of the noose. Then further back, to a warm summer's evening in a Nassau tavern. Jack grinning across at her, flushed with drink. She smiles. 'He said, "You can't hang us

75

all." ’

Anne slumps her head back against the wall, a snort of laughter tumbling out of her. ‘But they bloody well tried.’

‘Aye.’ Mary squeezes her hand. ‘That they did.’

‘Not all of us, though.’

Jack is dead. Charles Vane rots in a gibbet off Gun Cay, lashed with seaspray, his corpse a feast for the gulls. Or so the gloating guards have sniggered. Edward Teach is long dead. Benjamin Hornigold has disappeared, smashed upon rocks like that turncoat traitor deserves. Lawes is back in control now, overlord of all Jamaica, the *William* seized by the crown. Mary and Anne are creatures of the open sea, trapped too long in dungeons amid the sludge and muck of dreary hopelessness.

Mary remembers that quiet morning, bathed in golden sunlight amid the gentle murmur of the waves. ‘Not all of us. Not yet.’

Anne heaves a fond sigh, her thumb stroking Mary’s scarred knuckles. ‘We had some good times, didn’t we, sweetheart?’

Mary smiles back.

‘The best.’

STILL AS STONE

Our hostess prowls before us, like a hungry cat deciding which poor mouse to dine on first. We stare at the floor, dreading the prick of her sharp words like broken glass.

'No speaking.' We shudder at her stern tone. 'You are to be silent when guests arrive. Stay in character.' Her lip curls in disdain. 'You are invisible to my guests, and will remain so until *I* say otherwise.' The thin bamboo cane taps against her thigh. 'You know my rules; need I remind you of the penalty for breaking them?'

A muffled sob from the woman two spaces to my right, already half-dressed in grey robes. I can still glimpse the raw redness of her knuckles under the flickering oil lamps. I reach across and gently squeeze her injured hand. Her fingers tighten in mine.

Crack. A sharp, sudden pain; a line of white fire sears across my knuckles. I wrench my hand away, drop my gaze. The hostess's boots halt before me and her thin cane slides beneath my chin. Pressing upward. Raising my head. 'Ah, ah. Look at me.'

I keep my eyes fixed on the floor.

The voice hardens, edged with steel. '*Look at me.*'

I finally lift my gaze. The hostess stares back at me, cheeks flushed with rouge and her silver hair immaculately pinned back in a stern bun. She arches an eyebrow in amusement. 'Careful, now. Not going to be any trouble, are you?'

I hastily shake my head.

The hostess tuts and turns her back. 'I thought not. Well?' She claps her hands sharply; a collective shudder ripples along our line, like skittish foals at market. 'Carry on, then! Chop chop!'

I feel a sneeze brewing. The garden flowers are fragrant, lush … and full of pollen. Bugger. I sip shallow breaths until the urge passes.

Over by the sundial, Cupid sneezes. I wince in sympathy: that's half his pay docked. No leftover finger sandwiches for him, no port in a tiny thimble glass as the evening chill creeps in. The lady of this garden won't deign even a glance his way. To her, he's invisible.

As we all must be. And remain, until our hostess

orders otherwise. It isn't enough for her to have garden statues. To have a proper genteel party, they must be living statues.

Three of my neighbours are all dressed in the same grey, half-hidden in the shrubbery. Lady Liberty, her arm aloft bearing a flaming torch. Must be one hell of an elbow cramp. Sir Walter Raleigh, hands proudly on hips near the wisteria. Doesn't his ruff itch? Emperor Nero is frozen mid-oration by a stone vase, gazing into the middle distance. Strangers of both past and present; I don't know any of their names, only their disguises, and we never talk, anyway. Never meet each other's eyes. We just try not to breathe.

My elbow aches as I minutely adjust the parasol over one shoulder. Luckily my hat hides the worst of the sun's glare. A bee buzzes close and bumbles lazily around me; I cannot gasp or flinch. My gaze cannot flicker.

And I mustn't. Ever. Cough.

The bee drifts away toward the purple wisteria. The sun's blazing heat cracks the grey paint on my face. All for two shillings at day's end. Two bob. One loaf, an orange, two apples, a chicken, a handful of beans, milk, salt. The meagre price of keeping my stomach from growling. The paltry price of my dignity. I savour that chicken roasting in the oven, the salty crackle of crispy skin bursting on my tongue instead of the overpowering lavender that now clogs my nose.

A guest sits next to me. The chicken aroma shrivels away. Another plump guest arrives and they chat. Not with me. I'm merely an ornament. An idle decoration for a two-seater bench. The old tricks to aid my performance; eyes lowered to hide my blinking, hands loosely clasped so they won't sway or ache. But I cannot hide the bitter swell of shame, the tears that carve slow rivers of grey sludge down my burning cheeks.

The two strangers get up and leave; another wanders by. Slows. Sits. The mossy bench creaks under his bloated weight.

He leans close and nuzzles against my neck, crooning. Sausage fingers idly dance up my arm. I force down a shudder of revulsion. They might proclaim themselves refined gentlemen, but to me they're just fat, periwigged, perfumed pigs who waddle about the garden, reeking of brandy and port. The cream of high society? Snuffling about in the scrap trough, more like.

His splayed hand falls to my bare knee, fingers brushing the hem of my skirt. His other hand clasps my grey-painted wrist, moving it down onto his lap, towards his crotch. Sickening nausea crawls through my veins; a horrifying hardness presses against my palm, while close in my ear he grunts like a snuffling pig. Wine-soured breath washes over my face.

I could twist away. Wrench free. Turn and strike him down with the parasol. Batter him into the paving slabs with it.

But then I'd lose my job. My livelihood. Forced out to the workhouse, all for the sake of "some harmless sport". A pariah.

His thumb brushes my inner thigh. Inches higher. Higher –

Across the garden someone calls a name. He rises with a chortle and waddles off, disappearing through the shrubbery.

I breathe out. Long deep breaths, willing my hammering heart to still.

The hostess nods at me as she greets her guests, all smiles. She's pleased; I've done my job well.

When the last guest departs and I finally take my token two shillings, my employer hands me a nosegay of peonies, along with the tiny sandwiches and a worthless, craven simper. I take them without meeting her eye. Won't give her the satisfaction of gratitude. Her pitiful gifts won't nourish me. They aren't a reward. They won't fill my growling stomach. To me, they only smell of chicken.

81

Dusk. Two more near misses tonight, sweaty hands wandering wherever they please, groping where they shouldn't, my cheeks burning with shame, the bastards losing interest and wandering off for fresh distractions.

I'm Boudicca tonight, warrior queen and firebrand, shrouded in a flowing green dress belted with worn leather. Mercifully no grey body paint. Just my natural fiery red curls tumbling down my back. A cheap brass circlet pinches my skull. My right arm is held aloft in a frozen war cry. A heavy wooden hatchet in my hand. Blunted, of course. Pity.

The hostess glides through the bushes nearby. A faint trill of guests' laughter from the distant drawing room. The alluring scent of roast beef makes my mouth water. She pauses to smell a cluster of roses, plucks one out, wanders closer. Just the pair of us alone in this secluded haven.

Blood hisses through my ears, a rising tide of sizzling fury clawing against my ribs.

Enough. Enough of this disgrace. The crawling shame after each nauseating grope, after each disgusting pawing hand that wanders where it shouldn't. The debasing servitude as a token garden ornament. The petty humiliations. The indignities.

All for just two shillings a day.

No more.

One fateful blow. All it takes.

Maybe she'll cry out, struggle, alert the footmen. Bloodhounds baying after my scent, hooves thundering behind, horsemen swiftly surrounding me. I'll be caught before I've made it ten paces. A murderer paraded through the jeering crowd before I face the noose. Maybe it's futile. Maybe she'll scream.

Or maybe not.

My arm aches under the weight of the hatchet. No keen edge. Little more than a hefty bludgeon. Worse than useless.

Better than nothing.

The hostess drifts past, idly sniffing her rose. Out of view from the house. No one else to witness.

Behind her, unseen and unheard …

I raise the axe.

BURIED

I'm nearly blind down here. You get used to it.

It's dark down here. Darker than coal. Darker than Ma's furious eyes when I came home caked in mud after playing footer on the common. Which is before. A world of sunlight, trees, fresh air and laughter rolling on the breeze. When we weren't down here. Crouched in our tiny hollows beside the tracks, rope trailing between coal-blackened fingers. Waiting. Always waiting. And there's no oil left in the guttering Davy lamp. And there's rats. Scuffling around, pattering along the track. Chittering in the dark. Even sniffing at the bread and cheese in my pocket.

And they've filched it. And there's no point grumbling 'cause there's no one around to grumble at. Not till a hurrier comes along with a corf. But then there's the heavy wooden door that always needs opening. And closing again right away. Simple enough for a trapper like me, snug in my little alcove tucked into the wall, deep in the dank bowels of the earth. A quick heave of the rope, the door scrapes open and the metal coal cart clatters by with a fading call of 'Cheers, mate!'

And he's gone. Shut the door right away. Get it wrong and you get a clip round the ear, or a boot up the arse from the foreman later. A faint breeze slips through the closing gap, damp and earthy. Is it raining, far up the shaft? Is it raining, out under the open sky and the whispering trees? Must be. I haven't seen the sun in days.

Three more weeks before my seventh birthday in June. Maybe Ma'll bake a cake!

Maybe I'll get to see the sunrise. That'd be nice.

Until then, I settle down in the damp dark cold. To wait.

And wait.

And wait …

My back's killing me. No better than a carthorse with this harness round my waist. Digging into my shoulders. The chain that fixes to the corf goes taut. And I'm hunched, crawling on all fours where the ceiling's pressing low. Craggy rocks dig into my palms. The harness squeaks on rusty metal cinches, desperate for a smear of grease. I breathe in that chalky, stagnant stench of underground, like the old embers of a long-dead fire. The morning sun might scour the barren moors outside, burning off evening frost and morning mist alike. But here? Deep down? No chance of warming my frozen cheeks. I'm buried under mud and rock. My legs ache with cramp. And my arms are red raw.

But I'm used to it. I don't mind the cold. Or the loneliness, either. Or the dark yawning emptiness stretching before me. Only the black void keeps me company as I crawl on hands and knees like a babe, inch by inch, heaving that stubborn cartload of coal behind. Candle stubs flicker in the rockwork, sickly yellow light rippling off the rough-hewn walls like eddies in a pond. All alone down here, in the cold dark heart of the earth.

Not too bad, really.

Besides, they say being a hurrier is far better off than a thruster 'cause thrusters soon go bald from pushing the corf all day with their heads. Most of the men have thin patches now. Like Da. Ma always has his tin bath waiting for him back home, the water warmed by the same coals he blasted and carved from the earth, the same coals they paid him with. Two sackfuls that he lugs home every Friday. The comforting rattle as he pours them into the scuttle. A bonus, they called those coals. A pitman's hearthfire should never go cold.

Some days the exhaustion seeps so deep into his

bones he can barely hold his head upright. Doesn't stop him from taking a bath every afternoon. He'll stand in our tin tub by the fire, naked as a bridegroom on his wedding night, and scrub himself raw with a rag until his skin gleams. Then he'll offer the grubby rag to me with a crooked yellow grin.

'Do my back, lad?'

Someone's hammering on our front door. *Thump, thump, thump.*

I blink awake. There it is again: *thump thump thump.* Loud and urgent. The bedroom door clicks shut. Floorboards groan as Ma shuffles towards the door. In the gloom I grope for the curtain, pull it aside and peer through the frosty windowpane: a pale smudge of dawn seeps over the terraced rooftops opposite.

Our neighbour Maud huddles on the doorstep, shivering against the cold. My heart sinks. I claw back the sheets and tiptoe out the room. Ma opens the door.

'Edna,' Maud whimpers. 'Me man. He's missing down the mine. Yours too.' Her cheeks are wet with tears.

Ma sighs. 'C'mere, lass.' Maud crumples into her arms, weeping as Ma gently strokes her back;

huge heaving gasps shaking her to the bone.

'What'll I tell the bairns?' Maud whimpers into Ma's shoulder. 'How'll I cope by meself?'

Ma brushes a tear from her cheek. 'Easy now, Maud,' she murmurs. 'What happened?'

Between wretched gulping sobs Maud's story emerges; the workmen waiting at her door, bareheaded, twisting their caps in gnarled hands. The rumbling crunch they'd heard from the pit entrance. The pump beam collapsing, crashing down, choking up the mine's gaping maw. Faint echoes of distant prayers dribbling out of the darkness.

Ma lets out a shaky breath, rinsed with relief. Hope yet, for Tommy and the other two hundred poor souls trapped in the earth below our feet. An entire village's worth of husbands, fathers and sons buried down the yawning maw of the mine, awaiting rescue, praying to the Almighty for deliverance.

Maud pulls away, fidgeting with her shawl. 'The bairns ... I should ...'

We watch her wobble off down the garden path. Ma wraps an arm around my shoulders and shepherds me back indoors. 'C'mon, Jonny. Nowt we can do but wait.'

Two days later, there's still no word.

I potter around the house, adrift, aimless. Morning dawns, brightens into midday, fades into evening. Ma keeps her silent vigil, sitting at the kitchen window gazing out into dreary darkness. I scrape beef dripping over two slices of dry bread and leave one by her elbow. Nothing. She doesn't move, doesn't scream, doesn't rage around the kitchen in a storm of grief. She just sits. Watches. Waits.

Her food goes untouched. I feel the silence settle around us, dampening down like heavy snowfall, the stillborn quiet of an empty cottage. Holding its breath.

Knock knock knock.

I raise my head, eyes gluey with sleep. Ma is sitting upright amid rumpled sheets, nursing a mug of tea as she peers through the curtains.

'Jonny,' she breathes, groping for my shoulder. C'mon. Get up.'

Knock knock knock.

We shuffle down the hallway to the front door. My stomach curdles with dread. Ma fumbles with the latch, pulls it open.

A figure on the doorstep. Bob Tanner, the foreman. Broad-shouldered. Bareheaded. Cap twisting in his hands.

A huddle of workmen behind, bearing a stretcher between them. White cloth trails onto the cobbles. On it is –

The mug clatters to the floor. I watch the tea trickle out, soaking into the rug.

Ma sags against the door jamb. 'No,' she rasps. Her shoulders are rigid with tension, her eyes wide and dark. Refusing to believe it. 'He'll come back to us. He will. He's still alive …'

The leader scrubs a hand through his thinning hair. Meets her gaze. Shakes his head.

Ma lurches away from me, tottering down the hallway. Her eyes are glassy. Her shoulders slumped in defeat. She wanders away into the kitchen.

I stare down at the stretcher. At the body lying on it, shrouded all in white. A limp arm hangs down, fingertips brushing the cobblestones.

The scream echoes behind me, tearing through the pre-dawn hush like a shrieking gale; even though I'm expecting it, bracing for it, dreading it, it still rakes across my grimy skin and burns down to the roots of my teeth.

I learn, then, just how poisonous hope can be.

At last they've brought our Tommy home. Ma pulls me close and hugs me tight, weeping as they troop inside and lay him out on our kitchen table. I've never seen him so filthy. Those six days have left Da a hollow shadow of himself, black as the pit that choked the life from his lungs. Like all those broken bodies, all scattered limbs and mashed chitterlings deep underground until the earth finally vomited up its dead. But Da's skin is unmarked, untorn, smooth as glass; even after I peel off his foul work clothes, I can't find any freckle or scar beneath all that clinging soot.

'Do my back, lad?'

For the first time in over a week, Ma boils water by the panful, pouring it into the tub. Beside her the fire growls and coughs.

With shaky hands I sweep the old washcloth across his broad chest and watch the coal dust bleed from his grimy skin, trickling down his cold sides to pool in inky puddles beneath him. Somewhere beneath all that coal dust, my Da awaits. I only have to unearth him.

Ma says I'm the spitting image of Da. Meaning that I'm pale and scrawny like all the other men crowded at the coal seams, hacking away. And I'm always hungry. Although now I'm getting seven pence a day as a putter, we can maybe have ham and eggs for Sunday tea.

In the kitchen I take out the bread and jam, make a sandwich for the lunch pail, bread and jam each day, every day. Perhaps next week I'll fill the bread with ham instead. Little changes. The big ones seem too far out of reach. Billy's creased postcard lurks on the mantelpiece. He's a farmhand now. New Zealand. Toiling outside, soft grass under your feet, breathing in that sweet clean air. I've read and re-read every crooked line of his chicken-scratch handwriting, burning with envy how the sun on the back of his neck made him smile, made him feel "so completely alive."

Sod him.

We've nowt but feeble candles down here so the hewer can see the coalface. Pushing fifty at least. That wiry old dog looks it too. Wrinkled skin hangs from his bones like droopy sodden bedsheets; reedy blue veins thread all along his pale forearms. He turns and grunts at me: fetch something. I'm crouching down and scuttling around, picking up any loose nuggets of coal that tumble down as he chips away at the seam. And you can picture another world down there, lying just out of reach beyond the pitted black wall. Green fields, a rumbling breeze. Clouds drifting across endless eggshell blue, like glittering silver mackerel. Sometimes, I picture escape.

I'm twelve in July. Maybe I'll see the open sky.
For once.

The big day's here. My thirteenth birthday. And I'm
a proper man now. All grown up. With a pickaxe
slung over my shoulder which I lift and swing,
scrape, heave, knock the coals back to my putter
waiting behind. It's heavy work, being a hewer.
And the candles are flickering low again. And the
air tastes of liquorice. And I'm dog-tired so I close
my eyes. Not sure if I'm home snug in bed or still
down the pit.

I dream of Da's charred face in the darkness
that's darker than Ma's eyes. Says he wants to play
footer up on the common. Says it doesn't matter if
we go home all caked in mud. Or coal dust. Or
blood. As long as we get home on time. 'Cause
Ma's waiting with tea. Waiting all day from the
clanging bell that calls us in before sun up.
Entombed all day at the coalface. Hacking away.
Gouging deep into the bowels of the earth. The
darkness that's even darker than coal. My only light
is a guttering Davy lamp, its feeble light barely
seeping through the choking blackness.

Cramped legs. Squinting through the dark. A
crick in my neck from constant stooping. Arms
burned red raw. And for what? The mournful toll of

the bell as the pit haemorrhages men after each day's shift, yawning as we trudge wearily home to bed. Up again at the crack of dawn. Pausing to make the sign of the cross in front of Saint Barbara's china statue on the kitchen table. Bless my family. Bless me. Then the long walk into the darkness. Fifteen bob a week. Ham and eggs for Sunday tea.

The pit shelters its own secrets. Some days I travel to its secret belly, and before anyone on shift starts hammering with their tools, the earth breathes. A dull hum that you have to strain to hear. Like it's whispering only to us.

Tomorrow I'll spend Saturday playing footer in the field with Sam. Never after work. Too dark. Too tired. But tomorrow I'll show him how to kick the ball good and proper, so he'll get it exactly where he wants it. I'll savour the moment, keep Monday firmly out of mind. Tomorrow I'll feel the sun warm the back of my neck too.

Tomorrow.

HEART OF OAK

Shale crunches underfoot. Like bones snapping. Thomas Jopson jolts awake from his fever dreams, torn from a whispering darkness of gaunt-eyed phantoms and the creaking groans of a dying ship.

He dimly remembers the bawdy revelries last night – faint blurred half-memories of shouts and laughter and the rich scent of roasting meat as he'd drifted in and out of feverish semi-consciousness all that previous night – and he'd woken in the grey twilight to find that someone had left a plate bearing two forlorn strips of dripping white blubber, and a putrid slab of raw greasy seal meat. He'd retched – nothing had come up because he hadn't eaten for hours, days – and shoved the offending plate of offal out the half-open tent flap. Nothing but paltry scraps.

But now, with his insides scraped raw with hunger and his starving stomach growling for something, *anything* … he knows better. He was a fool to refuse.

He tries to roll over in his sodden sleeping bag, but he's swaddled tight like a newborn babe. Lightning bolts of pain burst through his skull. His ribs grind. His bones throb. He traces his tongue gingerly along the crooked ramparts of teeth. Dabs a forefinger over his tender gums, then stares puzzled at his bloody fingertip.

What's happening to me?

Muffled shouting. The dull grating scrape of wood grinding on rock. Blinking grit from his eyes he weakly raises his head and squints through the open tent flap, flinching back as a pale sliver of sunlight splashes his eyes like acid. He screws his eyes tight shut, but the after-glare burrows deep into his aching skull, fizzling deep into his brain. Harsh sunlight barely permeates the yellowed canvas walls, which heave and snap in the wind like the tanned hide of some great panting beast.

He peers out. Stares in disbelief. Ice crawls down his spine.

What in the world ...?

Thickly-clad seamen are clustered around a boat sledge some distance away, tightening straps and bracing themselves against the hull. A muffled call of 'Ready ... set ... *haul!*' and the men begin to move off. Dragging the boat behind them across the rocks. Out of the camp. The harsh, unbroken hiss of grinding shale fills the air.

Wait for me! For a brief flash of hope Jopson thinks he's shouted it aloud, but it's only a silent, desperate thought. He has to reach his crewmates … catch up to them before they shoved the boats further out onto the pack ice … heave himself into harness, loop the straps across his chest … show them that he could haul alongside the best of them. Perhaps he could fool them, pass muster by forcing down some of their reeking, rotten seal meat.

He looks across; a sickly crewmate gazes listlessly back from the opposite cot, his bloodshot eyes glazed beneath a matted curtain of greasy hair. Shallow rasping breaths dribble from cracked, windburned lips.

The awful truth sinks its claws deep, chilling Jopson to the bone. His despair is the howl of icy winds over scoured-bare jagged peaks. *I've been left here to die. They're leaving me behind. Forever.* Sickening bile rises afresh in his throat, but he forces it down. Wasn't his Naval record spotless? Wasn't he an excellent personal steward? Wasn't he a loyal upstanding citizen of Her Majesty as any other seaman on this doomed expedition? Did none of them give a damn? Why were they treating him like he was already dead? Boiling outrage scorches through him.

I won't stay here and die in this cold arse-end-of-the-world abandoned dump!

Straining with all his strength, he forces his Hudson's Bay sleeping bag down past his shoulders and begins creeping his way out of it. Hoarse rattling gasps echo in his ears from the glassy-eyed crewmate sprawled alongside.

Jopson ignores him. His numb mittened fingers scrabble desperately at the hard unforgiving shale as he crawls off the cot towards the tent flap, elbows scraped raw as his unfeeling legs trail behind. Like a low pathetic snail, a worm. Nothing more. Around him in the reeking gloom, bundled bodies grumble and groan like snoozing cattle. The stewed air inside the tent is ice cold against Jopson's cheeks as he drags himself along.

Twenty yards away the two remaining whaleboats are slowly moving off, rumbling over the sharp rocks as his crewmates plod wearily ahead. Towropes creak and strain as they haul the loaded sledges down the rocky beach, towards the endless expanse of frozen sea. Heads down. At least ten men per boat, perhaps more; all of the able-bodied survivors here at camp are leaving him behind. With the other sickly wretches barely clinging to life.

None of them look back. Not even a fleeting

glance.

Jopson stares after them, stricken with dread. *How can Dr Goodsir leave me behind?* He tries to remember when the surgeon had last lifted his head and shoulders to spoon another mouthful of lukewarm broth into his broken, rotted mouth, or wiped his feverish forehead with a damp rag. It was young Hartnell's turn yesterday, wasn't it? Or had that been several days ago? The memories curl up and shrivel away; he cannot recall the last time the surgeon had looked in on him or brought him medicine.

And now they are leaving him behind. Jopson stares outward at the departing figures hunched against their towropes. A boiling, blinding anger churning beneath his skin so intense it numbs his mind. Blood roars through his ears, pounding through his skull and bubbling with primal sizzling rage. Searing fury scorches through him, fizzling deep into his bones. His anger is a white-hot hissing sound between his ears like the whistle of an onrushing steam train, like a shrieking kettle, like a cornered rat snarling. It is a steel band wrapped tight around his chest, pounding hard against his ribs.

How dare they leave me behind?

Hadn't he stayed by Captain Crozier's bedside a

dozen, a hundred times during the captain's illnesses and moody bouts of depression and erratic bursts of drunkenness, the ever-patient loyal dog tending to his master, cooling his burning brow with a damp cloth? Hadn't he unflinchingly, uncomplainingly, like the good dedicated captain's steward he always was, hauled pails of stinking vomit from the captain's cabin and wiped the Irish drunkard's arse when he shat himself, sprawled out on his cabin floor in whisky-sodden deliriums? Hadn't he stayed by his bedside all night long and stroked the horrors away, like sluicing down a filthy mongrel that's been pulled whining from Regent's Canal? Hadn't he stripped the captain's sweat-soaked, bile-smelling sheets without complaint, carefully redressing him with a clean nightshirt and woollen socks to chase away the chills? Hadn't he nursed him for twelve long fitful nights before Crozier's fever finally broke and his crusted eyes cracked open like a newborn kitten's?

Perhaps that's why the bastard's leaving me to die. I've seen him in his most unguarded private moments, at his weakest, most vulnerable state.

And this is my reward. Left to rot in this godforsaken place.

There's nothing for it – he'll just have to crawl toward his able-bodied crewmates until they saw him and turned back. They wouldn't dare leave behind a fellow crewmate healthy enough to crawl a hundred yards after them onto the open ice.

Would they?

Jopson collapses forward through the tent flap and gasps as the sudden arctic chill claws at his parched throat. He's grown so accustomed to the canvas-filtered dim light and muggy stuffiness of his tent-womb, that the bleak openness and blinding sunlight make his lungs labour like worn bellows and his squinting eyes blur with tears.

But the sun's fierce glare is merely an illusion; the morning is dark and thickly fogged, tendrils of icy vapour drifting between the tents like the wandering spirits of all those dead seamen they'd left behind. Abandoned. Just like the thick fog on that fateful day they'd sent Lieutenant Little, Ice Master Reid, Harry Peglar and the others forward down the first open lead in the unforgiving, impassable ice.

To their deaths.

He gazes around; Rescue Camp looks deserted, except for a few low moans that could be issuing from nearby tents, or just a feeble echo of the incessant wind. The usual brisk crunch of boots on gravel, soft cursing, bursts of laughter, the mumbled small talk of men trudging to and from watch, cheerful shouts between tents, echoes of hammer or saw, the sharp tang of pipe tobacco – all are absent except for muffled and fading noises from the direction of the receding boats.

His breath hitches; lying outside his tent is a pile of rock-hard, half-green hardtack, along with three rusty Goldner tins. Rations stacked haphazardly by his tent like so many white rocks in preparation for burial. His only reward from years of faithful service to the Navy, to the Discovery Service and to Captain Crozier: a few lousy lumps of half-baked, fully stale ship's biscuit, and a handful of rotten tin cans. Brought to him as if he's some damned pagan idol or cheap sacrificial offering to whatever uncaring god leers down from on high.

His gaze slides wearily left and right, squinting through the fog towards the other two or three ragged tents still standing. Where are the rest? Why are they missing?

No. Not missing. Another handful of tents nearest the frozen shoreline are collapsed piles of rumpled canvas, with rocks tossed atop them to anchor them down. Doubt creeps through his veins; are his crewmates planning to return soon? If they truly meant to leave, why wouldn't they be taking the spare tents along with them? Where are they headed? Why? None of it makes any sense.

'W-wait!' he tries. It dribbles forth as a feeble croak from peeled frostbitten lips. How long has it been since he last spoke aloud? Days? Weeks, perhaps?

'Wait!' he calls again.

No one turns around. He is all alone. No one will come. He must pull himself along by his own willpower, haul himself after the receding men over rough stony ground. He claws for a large rock before him and, straining hard with all his failing strength, tries to urge himself on. Crawling on his belly like a snake, a pathetic maggot. All he hears is the slow scrape and grind of his broken body across the rocks, and the hollow roar of his own feeble panting. His dry palms scrape over jagged stone, freezing shale burning his worn flesh as he creeps forward, slowly and painfully.

One inch. Two. Three.

He digs his right elbow into the unforgiving shale. Then his left. Gains an extra inch. He is dripping sweat, his lungs wheezing and roaring inside his chest like tattered bellows in an iron forge. He forces himself onward, gasping with the ungodly effort of dragging his body across the pitiless rocks after the departing men. His hands clutching at sharp handfuls of shale.

'Wait!' That's no better. He has to raise himself

up somehow, wave his arm in the air, make them notice him, make them turn back for him. He struggles to prop himself up, pain slicing through his numbed limbs.

His elbow slips away, he crumples sideways and his jaw slams down heavily onto the shale. He rolls over with a groan. Spits out a cracked tooth. His heartbeat is like a heavy oaken door somewhere far off in the distant mist being slammed hard, over and over again. He grits his teeth, and gradually the shrill pain lessens into a dull nauseating ache. The sledge party are fading further and further away.

Jopson wriggles forward on his torn elbows another three feet and collapses facedown onto the icy gravel, panting for breath. The fog roils around him, obscuring even his own tent only a few paces behind him. The wind moans – or perhaps just the ghoulish echo of more abandoned souls in the few ragged tents still standing – and the arctic chill sinks right through his filthy shirt and soiled britches. A rush of icy dread; if he keeps crawling away from his sickbay tent, he might not have the strength left to crawl back inside, and would die of cold and damp out here on the pitiless rocks.

He cracks open parched wind-burnt lips and calls 'Wait!' but his voice is now as weak and mewling as a newborn kitten's. He crawls and wriggles and writhes another two feet. Three. Four. He lies gasping like a harpooned seal, utterly spent. His weakened, dragging arms and hands are of no more use than flippers would be. Of less use, even. Worthless.

He tries digging his chin into the frozen earth to propel himself forward another foot or two. A lancing jolt of pain as one of his last remaining teeth chips against a stone. He digs his chin in again for another try. His body is simply too heavy, too cumbersome, anchored to the earth by huge leaden weights. Impossible to move.

'Wait … wait … wait … wait.' Each croak is fainter than the last. Panting, gasping, his remaining strands of hair dabbing crimson streaks onto the jagged stones, Jopson lies on his belly, deadened arms at his sides, and rests his cheek against the cold hard shale so that he can squint ahead.

The fog swirls and lifts.

He stares, scarcely believing his eyes: white linen tablecloth stretches out before him, endless, like some ice laden path to nowhere. A huge banqueting table is spread before his eyes, laden with a sumptuous feast. Saliva drips unbidden from his parched lips, for the most extravagant dishes his delirious imagination can conjure are covering the table: pheasant, succulent roast pork, boiled calf's head, larded oysters, Florentine of rabbit, citrus ice, custard pies, meringues floating in crème anglaise. Steamed puddings jostle for space alongside wobbling jellies, and heaped bowls of trifle nudge broad silver platters of roast potatoes. Brandy and whisky are lined up in their sparkling cut-crystal decanters, like proud soldiers on parade.

But Jopson only has eyes for the figure seated at the head of the banquet table: Captain Francis Crozier, comfortable, well-fed and bathed in luxury chatting away silently to an invisible guest beside him. Utterly indifferent to his ailing steward's suffering.

'C-Captain!' Dismay curdles in Jopson's belly. He crawls across the rumpled tablecloth shoving lavish delicacies aside, urging his body onward … but Crozier continues nattering away, surrounded by decadence, oblivious to his desperate pleas.

'Captain …'

The vision shrivels and fades; Jopson is sprawled across the rocks as the able-bodied seamen disappear below the hillside with their boats. Not a single man looks back at him.

He is shuddering with cold, and he feels his sweat-soaked clothes beginning to harden around him like a coat of heavy chainmail. His lungs and throat ache from the arctic chill; his palms scraped raw and bleeding; he is panting, rasping for air, with blood thrumming in his ears.

'Wait!' This last shout has taken his last ounce of draining energy – Jopson can feel his body's warmth seeping away into the icy ground beneath him – but it spews forth as loud as any spoken word he has ever uttered.

'Wait!' he finally shouts; a man's voice now, not a kitten's mewl or dying seal's squeak.

But it's far too late. The men and boats are now over a hundred yards out and receding fast – their retreating backs are merely black, staggering silhouettes diminishing against an endless expanse of shifting grey – and the scraping and groaning of ice and wind would cover even the loud crack of a rifle shot, much less the feeble solitary bleating of one man left behind. Forgotten. Abandoned.

For an instant the fog lifts and a benevolent light washes over him – as if the sun were finally coming out to melt the ice everywhere and to bring forth green tendrils and living things and hope back into this desolate barren hellscape where none dared exist here before – but then the smothering fog closes in and swirls around Jopson, blinding and binding him with its clammy, cold grey fingers. The grey sea floods around him, silent and empty.

And then the men and the boats are gone. Forever.

As if they'd never even existed.

All his hard work and love … worthless.

Not even a single goodbye spared from anyone.

Jopson's eyes cloud with bitter tears. He is alone. In a vast emptiness paved with unforgiving shale and canopied with dull grey sky. Completely and utterly alone in the middle of nowhere, cast off like useless flotsam. Smeared by cloud, the sun gives off no discernible heat. He has crawled too far after a hopeless cause, he knows that now: dragged himself after his deaf comrades, sloughing off another thin skin of civilisation with every painful inch, until there's nothing left to give.

He has strayed from his true purpose, lost and bewildered, and his failure is complete.

With a groan of despair he drags himself around, inch by excruciating inch, and begins the slow shameful retreat back to the stewed warmth of his sickbay tent. For a moment he gazes up at the white indifferent sky, then, dazed and helpless, he slumps down onto the rocks and closes his eyes.

'The men will have their say, of course.'

Jopson's voice is a dry, rasping croak. His throat is scratchy and raw; for weeks he hasn't spoken more than five words stringed together. Now the words have begun, they're spilling forth from his rotten mouth like a dam crumbling.

'The weakest will have first choice; whichever cut suits each man best. I don't know who's taken over cooking, but they'll fend for themselves. I will take whatever scraps are left. No deference to rank here. No pecking order. Not anymore.'

He gazes from his tent flap out over the limestone shale where it blends into the dreary grey sky. The sunlight is blinding, and he squints to better glimpse the men who shuffle aimlessly from hovel to sledge to firepit. They barely acknowledge one another as they wander around the bleak camp. So few left now, and each has been whittled down to pathetic desiccated shells, hollow-eyed ghosts of their former selves. The gnawing aches in their broken bodies, tottering along like splintered glass.

Jopson attempts to swallow. His bloated tongue clogs his mouth, and he fights back a cough. The untouched Goldner tins moulder before him. He'll be damned if he eats from them, and damned if he doesn't. Those tins that are not spoiled are poisoned, have been poisoned since the beginning.

No seabirds or prey worth snagging, not in this endless grey nothingness. They are doomed.

'We still eat,' he mumbles, turning his gaze once

again to the salt-crusted greatcoat in his hands. He clenches his fist around it, bunching the material until his fingers quake. There's a speck of yellow vomit near his thumb by the woollen collar. 'We still eat. The butchering takes more from me than the relief I get from the meal. But still we eat. It's something to do. Passes the time.' He stops. 'Who made that first decision? When we ate Young. Was it you? Did *I* make that command? Did we have them vote?'

He turns his bleary gaze to William Gibson, who lies unmoving in his bedroll staring unseeingly at the ragged tarp canvas above. No answer. Jopson feels a sizzling pain growing behind his eyes, a sour sickness curdling in his stomach. Talking to Gibson is like shouting into the darkness and expecting the darkness to answer back in kind. He clears his throat, fighting down another cough.

'It's been so long that … I can't remember.' He rubs at the vomit marring the coat, nose wrinkling from the unpleasant odour. No worse than the stench from his own rancid body, his filthy clothes, or the acrid stink wafting from Gibson, from the stain seeping into his bedclothes and draining onto the rocky ground beneath him.

Snarls from outside. A fight breaks out at the fire pit; two ragged wretches are nose to nose, their voices loud and discordant. They exchange a few flailing blows, clawing at each other's grimy shirts; but before Jopson can rise, can even croak a warning at them, they slump bone-weary against each other. They're panting hard, heads drooped to their chests, arms dangling limp.

'No, I don't remember,' Jopson murmurs, watching the men resettle, huddled around the fire as though there wasn't a fight barely moments ago. 'Don't suppose it matters anymore. What good's a vote now, anyway?'

No response from the corpse alongside him. He crawls on his hands and knees across the tent, picks up his jackknife and rubs his thumb over the blade. Hunger gnaws at him, raking his insides with its insistent claws. He thinks of the meat under his knife, ready for carving – fresh, red – and feels the drool begin to puddle in his mouth.

He bows his head, face flushed with shame. 'I'm not a monster, you understand? If there were another way I'd take it, you know that.' His voice is a feeble, pleading whine, pathetic even to his own ringing ears.

'But I'm hungry. And … and I want to *live*.'

He gropes for Gibson's limp arm, pulls it towards himself, and grimly gets to work.

It's not like carving up a pig, that pink succulent meat marbled through with fat. Nor a duck, that lean earthy meat browned with gravy, almost melting off the bone. Nor even like skinning a rabbit, or adding chunks of tough mutton for the stewpot. The flesh is leathery, greasy, dense and grey, reeking of sweat. It does not want to go, but the reluctant struggle it puts up is weak under a knife, even one as dulled as this.

The effort leaves him exhausted; it would be far easier with a sharper knife or a healthier cadaver, neither of which he has.

Meat and gristle, he tells himself. Just meat and gristle. He saws the knife back and forth, back and forth until the first sliver of meat jolts loose.

He lifts the ragged grey morsel to his lips with trembling fingers, and begins swallowing down his humanity, swallowing down the shadow of a man.

He saws and he carves and he slices. He chews and he tastes and he cries.

And cries.

And cries.

He keeps the head. He props it against the crate.

There is a fascinating – if disgusting – irony that Gibson should watch Jopson as he eats raw slivers sawed from his thigh, his bones scraped clean of meat with a blunt jackknife and now bleaching in the wind. Some perverse, twisted justice. Jopson doesn't eat much. His stomach has shrunk to a withered husk, and he cannot bear more than a few meagre chews. He covers the plate with a cloth, saving the meat for later, and wraps his threadbare blanket around his shoulders to watch the brief sunset.

'Do you think the captain still lives? I hope he doesn't, if I'm honest. Not now, anyway. If living's like this –' He pauses, unsure how to continue, but he assumes Gibson understands. The dead always do. 'It's hardly living. Surviving. Scraping the earth. This is Hell.'

In a couple hours' time, the sun will rise again, and the men in the camp will continue their mindless shuffling circuit over the limestone.

His cracked fob-watch, once used to measure between mealtimes, now counts the crawling hours until the next dreary sunset, until the biting cold of oncoming night. The daylight hours are lengthening now, it's true. But all that serves is to illuminate the stark, desolate nothingness surrounding them on every side. A blasted wasteland of ice and rock where nothing grows, crawls or sings. A leaden grey sky utterly free of clouds and seabirds.

And the corpses will remain frozen hard in their

sleeping-bag shrouds, contorted into the terrible clawing visages of their final death throes. They haven't broken camp in over a week. Even the men that trudge around the perimeter in a mockery of sentry watch only do so to stem the hunger pangs at bay, to keep their leaden legs limber. Without the usual healthy rigor of their shipboard duties, they have grown listless and pale; the cold and gnawing starvation has sapped the dwindling strength from their bones. Empty tins litter the campsite, their putrid sludge shovelled with trembling frostbitten fingers into ash-grey mouths rotted from scurvy.

What will the poets say, in long years hence? That they were Englishmen to the very end? That they endured, as was their duty? For England. For God and country. As any man must?

No. Not endure. Survive. Clawing their way up from the lowest depths of Hell, for another brief glimpse of pale uncaring sun. They are men no longer. Just savage beasts.

'What do you think the Admiralty's doing?' It's a dangerous thought, but Jopson feels a sudden flare of desperate energy, manic fervour gripping him as the hope smothers him in an iron stranglehold. 'Are they searching for us? Do they know we yet live?'

He lapses into glum silence, watching the sky darken; not enough for stars to glimmer but enough that the air loses some of its dreary glow, shadows deepening inside the ramshackle tent until the chill bites into Jopson's bones. But the thought of rescue sustains him as he daydreams how they might be discovered, how a ship of whalers might find them on this barren coastline of King William Land, this desolate rocky sunless wasteland where nothing walks or grows or lives. Perhaps by some great miracle they would have found Captain Crozier alive and well. The men would convalesce on ship as they returned home to England, never to sail in these icy Arctic waters again.

One day ...

The glaring sunrise pricks his eyes, and the dream shrivels away. Jopson sighs. He leans back against the crate, wraps the blanket tighter around himself, and closes his eyes. Tomorrow, he'll rise from the heavy clinging fog of sleep, open his rheumy eyes to the same stark, dull horror that awaits.

'Do you think our families miss us?' he mutters, unsure from what hidden well of grief inside him that question comes. 'Did you have sisters? Brothers? I can't ... I can't even remember what my own mother looks like.' He chokes down a sob. 'Her hair. Her eyes. I can't remember ...'

He is suddenly grateful that he sleeps alone in

this tent, alone except for Gibson's head, that no man living should see him weep into his hands, repeating *I can't remember, I can't remember*. He marshals himself; he will not bemoan his grievances anymore for Gibson. No. No more sulking like a spoiled child.

He lets the memories die inside his mouth instead. Crumbling to ash on his tongue.

'Hopeless,' he whispers. 'Fucking hopeless.'

A Netsilik family strays near their squalid camp next sunrise. They pause at the crest of the hill, wary of the white men's camp. Jopson watches from his tent as two emaciated seamen approach the family. He hears nothing of the conversation, but it's short. The men shuffle back to camp, dejected in spite of the fresh seal meat gifted to them. It's not enough to share; Jopson half expects the men hunched around the fire to begin tearing into each other like rabid dogs, fighting over pitiful handfuls of meat.

But the two men hoard it amongst themselves. They cram the slimy meat into their pockets, greedily hide it from their crewmates, perhaps waiting for a chance when they may eat in private and luxuriate in the taste of something other than raw flesh or the rancid clumps of tasteless sludge spooned from rusty tins into broken mouths. Or the rock-hard mouldy lumps crawling with weevils that the Admiralty had the nerve to call 'biscuits'.

The next morning, both bodies lie dead by the lifeboat, stripped naked for butchering.

They don't belong here. They never did. He still hears dead sailors' whispers in the wind, the creaking groan of ice grinding against a dying ship's splintered hull, the feeble hiss of oil lamps struggling to fight off the relentless cold. Men reduced to savage beasts sucking the flesh from each other's bones. A black stain on their souls, one sunk far too deep to scrub out, one that no amount of blinding polar sun could ever bleach away.

First Young. Then Hodgson. Then Armitage, and Rogers, and … once they started, they couldn't stop themselves. Gnawing away like starving rats.

'Will we ever be forgiven? For all … this?'

He worries the gold chain between his fingertips where he keeps it stashed deep in his pocket, where the warmth of his body keeps the metal tolerable.

'Does God even know we're here?' He glances at Gibson. The head is tilted to one side, his silver hair matted with dirt, one eyelid drooping where the eye has rotted. Jopson turns away with a grumble, 'What would *you* know? I'd ask Crozier, were he here.' His throat grows tight, thinking of

Francis. He turns his angry glare back to Gibson. 'Who the hell *are* you to me? Another brother officer? A crewmate? A *friend?*' He spits the word like filth. 'No, you pompous selfish bastard, Francis was my friend. James was my friend.' His voice catches. 'Edward was my friend. Crozier, Fitzjames, Little … None of them are here now. Only me and you … and this *goddamned bloody Arctic!*' His roar is loud enough that he hears the despondent echo rattle through the camp. No one bothers them, numbed now to Jopson's furious tirades, his mutterings to ghosts long gone, long dead. 'No one's coming. We're already dead, Will. The captains are dead. Sir John is dead. You're dead. I'm dead. We've already been damned to Hell. Forevermore.'

He scrambles up, seething, and kicks the head away. Watches it scrape and tumble over the shale until it rests a few feet off.

He feels wetness on his cheeks. Tastes salt in his beard. He takes his hand from his pocket and covers his face, sobbing like a blubbering child. He crawls on all fours to Gibson's head, gentle as he picks it up, cradles it. Uses his sleeve to wipe dust from Gibson's cheeks, runs his fingers through the ash-grey hair so it flops with a familiar curl over his forehead. The nose is broken – from what and

118

when, Jopson cannot say – but he leaves it alone. He props the head against the crate and huddles away from it.

He shakes his head. 'I know, I know. I'm sorry. It isn't your fault.' He slips his hand back into his pocket, stroking the gold pocketwatch chain with his fingertips. 'I know, I know. I'm sorry. I'm so sorry.'

Distantly he feels his stomach clench from hunger, and pulls the plate toward him. The meat is darkening, discoloured at the edges, already fading to grey. He cannot remember how long it has stewed there on the plate, but he raises a ragged morsel to his lips, chewing through leathery toughness.

He can no longer taste, he realises, and swallows with difficulty.

He looks to the heavens, imagining for a moment that the sky is more blue than grey, that the sun moves more than a lazy half-circle above their cursed heads. His laboured breaths are the death rattle of a starving wretch, a shrunken pathetic beast groaning in desperation into the indifferent arctic wind.

'Do you think any leads will open up in spring?' he asks Gibson beside him. 'That we might sail further west? Find the Passage?' The head doesn't answer, just a vacant one-eyed stare of *I know something you don't know*. Jopson takes another bite of flavourless meat. It does not nourish him. Never will. 'We are close, I think. Very close.'

It comes for him just after midnight.

Jopson feels the numbing, gnawing pain creeping up his legs, tingling his mittened fingers which tighten around his double-barrelled shotgun.

Birdshot, that's all. For netting seabirds. Bloody useless against what's been stalking them – *him* – for days now. A humped shadow on the ridge. Snow crunching beneath monstrous paws. A rumbling growl in the night, fading into silence. Relentless. Ravenous. Patiently biding its time.

A few stars glimmer in the twilight. A cutting wind slices in from the northwest, like it always does in the evenings, and the temperature has plummeted from its noontime high just above freezing. Jopson hunkers down amid the forlorn wreckage of the lifeboat. The only remnant of *Terror* groaning out its death throes in the merciless ice. How long has it been since they abandoned ship and trudged into oblivion? Two weeks? Five days?

His messmates lie strewn about like windblown leaves, curled up as if asleep, waxen blueish faces relaxed into sweetness. John Bates, who would never bawl another sea shanty from Terror's yardarm again. Henry Sait, who would never again snigger at Will Jerry's smutty jokes, eyes twinkling over his can of salt pork.

Here, on the far edge of the world, beneath an uncaring sky, is where their end will find them. A quick ending would be a kindness, but there is no mercy to be found in this desolate hellscape. One by one, faded in body and spirit, the other wretched seamen have retreated to the crude shelter of the lifeboat, huddling together like orphans with eyes closed as if this is all a bad dream from which they might awaken from. The field promotion to Lieutenant, the gold braid on his shoulder hasn't meant much in the end, but he can still do this. He can still keep watch over his men. He props himself up against their last barrel of frozen water, shotgun at hand, waiting for what follows them.

The dead come to him. All those men left abandoned and betrayed. He sees John Kenley's gaunt-faced stare, the quartermaster's frostbitten hands held out before him, forcing Jopson to bear witness. And behind Kenley every other wretch cast aside like so much unwanted baggage, like useless deadweight. Men they had left sleeping by the wayside, hoping they would never wake. He

121

sees Henry Sait collapse into a groaning heap on the unforgiving shale, the old stoker William Johnson casting off help to lift him up, bearing the younger man across stones that crunch like old bones beneath his fraying boots; a bridegroom with his rotting bride. He sees Fitzjames. He sees Crozier. Other men fade into view, shadowy strangers whose names he's long forgotten.

The dead have no words for him. They gather around him, staring and silent. No noise now but the frigid wind rattling the ramshackle lean-tos and Jopson's own rasping breaths. Nothing here but Jopson. And the watchful voiceless dead.

His empty stomach claws at him. And suddenly the beast is just *there*! Looming up on the pack-ice not thirty paces from him. Must have swum up from some invisible breathing hole and crept in for the kill. Jopson squints at it from the itchy depths of his woollen balaclava.

'Yer late.' He smiles at the shadowy silhouette. 'What in the name o' God took ye so fuckin' long?' The bear rears up on massive shaggy hindquarters, a huge snow-white mass of fur and muscle and vicious ripping claws and a faint gleam of primeval teeth way back in mankind's memory. More than ten feet tall. Perhaps twelve. No dying sunlight glints in its malevolent slate-black eyes. Just pitiless slits of endless darkness.

'Welcome back,' Jopson mumbles. He can't help his teeth from chattering. 'I've been waitin' for you.' He claws for an empty tin can and hurls it at the monster. The crude missile doesn't even make five yards. Just flops into the snow with a wet squelch. Pathetic.

The nightmare towers there, implacable, then drops onto all fours. Begins circling. A growl bubbling from bared fangs. No witnesses. No songs or tales whispered down the years. Just a dying man facing his bitter end at the arse end of frozen Hell, cornered by a ravenous man-eater.

Jopson's eyes drift up to the twisted words carved into the lifeboat's shattered ribs, some little more than weak scratchings of despair, others deeply scoured out in delirious rage. *Goodbye Jenny ... Forgive us, Lord ... Gone. All gone ...*

And scrawled across the splintered gunwale in crude Latin: *Morior invictus.*

Death before defeat.

Jopson clenches his jaw. A fierce rush of scorn rises in his heart. No. No, he won't slip away into eternal night leaving this scavenger to feast on his mates. To Hell with that. He'll make it bleed for them first.

He squeezes the trigger and the shotgun roars,

jolting his numb shoulder. A harmless spray of snow spatters the creature. Missed. It pauses, mud-streaked hide bristling with rage. A trickle of blood mats its fur, dripping down its foreleg. A lucky stray pellet that found its mark.

A rush of triumph seeps through Jopson's deadened bones. If he can wound it, he can hurt it. If he can hurt it, he can kill it. An empty shotgun and a blunted pigsticker? Fat chance of that.

But still – no harm in trying.

'Yeah?' Jopson smirks, groping for his jackknife. He fumbles it open with frozen fingers. 'You're an evil-lookin' bastard, aren't you? Well … I'm armed, with a –' he falters, then rallies, '– a knife! *Heh*? So … I'll understand if you want to *run away now*.' Maybe two or three frenzied stabs into the base of its skull; when all else fails, go for the eyes. But for that, he'll have to let it get up close.

Real close.

Oh well. Not like he's got anywhere else to be. Here's as good a place as any.

Jopson clenches his jaw. No going out in a gibbering, whimpering shitheap of terror. If he's to die, it won't be crippled with blindness and gnawing fear. If he's to die tonight, he'll go down fighting. Spitting in Death's face.

If he's to die, it's going to be a bloody, glorious,

spectacular mess.

White furry bastard wants him gone good and proper? Wants to feast on his bones? It can damn well put the work in.

'Fuck you,' he growls, goading it on. Spreads his arms wide. 'C'monnn, you fuckin' coward. Eh? Come at me. I'm *right here!*'

It snarls and rushes forward like a wraith, paws thundering the ice, a monstrous mass lunging rapidly towards him across the frozen wastes, its dark terrible solidity finally opening arms to fill the steward's squinting vision. It looms over his broken body.

Jopson bares rotten teeth and smirks up into his death's merciless face.

'I hope I give you the shits, you fuckin' *wimp*.'

It *roars* into his face. Drool splatters his cheeks, a hot reeking stench washing over him.

His blood hissing in anticipation, Jopson cackles fiercely and raises his knife for the last time.

ONE SHOT

He'll be twenty-seven in just two weeks, but he won't live to see his birthday.

He doesn't plan to.

The thick Turkish carpets muffle his footsteps as he walks, his polished spurs glinting under the hissing gas lamps. A few dawdlers glance his way; the gentlemen smile or nod, the ladies simper and giggle behind their fans. His dark ensemble might raise a few eyebrows – hardly appropriate evening-wear for a night like this – but none challenge him.

Why should they? Tall and slim with brown curly hair, he cuts a dapper figure tonight in a smart black suit, frock coat and knee-high cavalry boots. Besides, he's familiar here. Night after night he struts and frets his hour upon the stage, serenaded with rapturous applause and roses flung by adoring ladies. His audience love him. Some even revere him. Nobody suspects a thing.

Fools.

Up the stairs, along the corridor. A faint

smattering of applause, ripples of laughter; somewhere in Act III? Mustn't dawdle. Time's ticking on.

He slips his hand into his pocket, fingers curling around smooth walnut and cold metal. His snug little Derringer. Only one shot.

One is enough.

Fathers. Sons. Brothers. Cousins. An entire generation snatched into oblivion by steel, shrapnel and cannon-fire, swallowed up by the endless crushing tide of Union blue. Thousands of lost souls clamouring for retribution, their ghosts sighing among the sweltering bayous of Louisiana and the cotton fields of Alabama, white as new-fallen snow. Never again would they tramp over the rolling meadows of Georgia, nor reap the golden cornfields of Tennessee.

Everything is ready. The stage is set. The players all know their parts, to slay the three-headed dragon of the North. Lewis Powell will go after Seward. George Atzerodt will pursue Johnson.

But his target? The greatest prize of all.

Vengeance is mine, sayeth the Lord.

Ah, here it is. Last door on the left. He pauses to compose himself, the Bowie knife heavy on his left hip. Things could turn ugly. He hopes not.

But: plan for the worst.

Three. Two. One.

Weapons drawn, he slips inside.

Four places are occupied. Furthest to his right, a heavyset uniformed man reclines on the settee with his fiancée, his epaulettes and brass buttons gleaming under the stage lights. Beside them, closer, a stout woman in bonnet and evening gown eases back in her chair with a creak of wickerwork.

And nearest the door, barely two paces away in a plush red rocking chair …

He shivers. Abraham Africanus the First, in the flesh. The famous sideburns and beard, a full head and shoulders taller than his high-backed chair. Over a month since he last stood behind the tyrant, under a chilly March sky facing a sea of thousands with his reedy voice echoing over the crowd. *'Malice toward none, with charity for all …'*

Tell that to the mothers, widows and orphans left crying in the dark. Richmond swallowed in hellfire, night sky torn asunder as the shells screamed down. Limbless cripples pleading for quarters in the gutter. A shroud of grief over every Memphis street. The curtains drawn, the mourning wreaths on every door, the widows veiled in black crepe. All their boys in grey who marched away singing, and never came home again.

A ripple of laughter through the crowd, echoed

by a comedic blast from the brass section. Unheard in the hubbub, he clicks back the hammer.

All or nothing. He walked in tonight, head high. He won't be walking back out.

But: hope for the best.

Below, a man dressed in drag prowls across the stage. 'Guess I know enough to turn you inside out, old gal … you sockdologizing old man-trap!'

The tyrant rocks forward, shaking with laughter as his guests guffaw beside him.

Behind them in the gloom, a silent shadow steps forward.

For the South, John Wilkes Booth thinks, and raises his pistol.

WHITEWASH

The teacher rummages around inside his top hat, eyes lidded in suspense. Finally, he whips out a white rabbit and chortles.

Nobody laughs. Thirty stony faces glare back at him. Sullen defiance is all we can manage, since they herded us within these walls like bison. They hammered up internment camps in red, white and blue, and called them schools. Filled them with mouthless faces stripped of all colour, and called us pupils.

Off came our tribal beads, our sacred feathers, our buckskin dresses, our soft-soled moccasins that still smelled of home. We wept as cruel scissors snipped away, pricking our scalps, our flowing locks littering the ground like dead crows. They imprisoned us in tight grey tunics and pale shirts, choking collars chafing our necks raw, buttoned cuffs shackling us. The hard leather boots pinched our toes. No laughter here, free and wild like the endless rolling plains. Just the mournful toll of the lunch bell, the tramp of hundreds of feet, the scratch of pen on paper.

And the stinging snap of the cane. Over tiny knuckles, over quaking palms, over trembling buttocks, for not speaking the language. White Bull. Little Wolf. Running Bear. Pretty Eagle. All marched in for their punishment, heads high and proud warriors, and came back shrunken and flinching at shadows, fresh raw welts reddening across their palms. *English*, the white-skins scolded us, *speak English now. None of you savages here.* We knew what it was like to hurt – but not the word for *help*.

They beat us. Starved us. Scorned us. Stole us from ourselves. And yet … they call *us* savages?

SUFFRAGETTE

Blood hisses through her ears as she edges along the corridor. It's a small dingy flat, and the floorboards creak … the front door is only five paces away now … if she can just …

Beneath her foot a board groans. Her heart sinks.

'Rose?' A door creaks open; lamplight spills into the hallway. Frank appears frowning in the doorway, boot polish in one hand and blackened leather boot in the other. 'Jenny's snorin' upstairs – where're you sneaking off to, luv?'

She exhales, pastes a cheery grin across her face and turns towards him. 'Just off to Maud's!' she lies. 'Wanted to thank her for sending us that cake!'

Frank grins, uncertainty melting away into placid relief. 'Right. Give 'er my love, won't you?'

'Will do!' she lies, pulling the front door shut behind her.

Outside the evening chill washes over her. In the shadow of the porch she breathes out; she isn't meeting Maud at all. Never planned to. But what

Frank doesn't know won't hurt him. Or Jenny. Far safer that way.

She unfolds the scrap of paper clutched in her fist, re-reads it then scurries off into the night drizzle, collar up and head down. Her hardwood Indian club is a solid reassuring weight concealed in her handbag, polished ash the size of a hefty bowling pin.

A cat yowls nearby, a bottle tinkles and she turns automatically to check behind her. Nothing but the deserted street, barred with shadow and bathed in orange lamplight. Rats rustle in a row of three lidless bins. She hasn't lost her own habit of ceaseless watchfulness. Imperative in these troubled times; she's written articles on the subject. Better safe than sorry.

For those of us in constant danger of re-arrest, vigilance is key. Are you sure the fellow walking up your garden path is the usual postman, or might he secretly be a plain-clothed policeman? That ordinary cove peering into a shop window across the street – is it possible he's eyeing your reflection instead? Be like two-faced Janus – look before and behind at all times, always aware; be like Argus, giant with a hundred watchful eyes.

Shallow puddles glisten under the misty glow of amber street lamps. As she nears her destination she slips into the shadow of an alleyway. Scans the empty street. Left. Right. Left again.

All clear.

She darts across the road and sidles up to the door, tapping out the secret passcode while her heart hammers against her ribs. Two knocks. Pause. One knock. Pause. Three quick knocks.

Floorboards creak within. Bolts scrape back. Lamplight washes over her and hands quickly haul her inside. The door swings shut on oiled hinges.

Molly clasps her hands, her freckled cheeks beaming. 'Thank goodness you made it! C'mon!' She leads Rose down the dim corridor to the inner sanctum where a circle of seated women await, faces alight with purpose. Ribbons and rosettes, medals and badges wink from bosoms and lapels; Emma's living room currently seats more convicted criminals than a lively East End beer-hall.

Rose gazes around at her old comrades with a swell of fond pride: Grace the leaflet-maker, her pinched sallow face creased in a mild grimace as she sucks a peppermint, the bag rustling in her lap. Treasurer Liz, plump-cheeked and eyes twinkling beneath her dark crown of curls. Their grey-haired ringleader Emma lends genteel respectability to the cause. She wears her purple, green and white sash and her Holloway brooch proudly, but not the silver pin bearing her hunger strike dates. ('I've no wish to look like the crusty old veteran of a forgotten war,' she's insisted in past meetings. 'The battle's not yet over; every day brings fresh skirmishes.')

She stands and gazes around the circle like a benevolent headmistress addressing nervous first-term schoolgirls. 'Evening, ladies. Tonight I'd like to welcome our newest sister-in-arms to the cause.' She turns to a fidgety dark-haired young girl whose hands twist in her lap. 'Laura?'

The girl shrinks into herself. 'Hi,' she mumbles.

Emma beckons her forward. 'C'mon, lass, it's okay. You're among friends. Tell us your story.'

Laura rises with obvious reluctance, eyes darting around the smiling group like a cornered rabbit. A reassuring pat on the back from Emma, a gentle smile from Molly and her words begin to trickle out, haltingly at first then slowly gathering strength. Her story is nearly identical to Rose, who winces in sympathy. Toiling from dawn till dusk at the Glasshouse Laundry in Bethnal Green. Ironing in a steam-clouded room, the walls pearled with damp, piles of folded linen that couldn't ever be touched or even brushed against, her and her workmates edging crab-wise across the room, arms pressed to their sides. Her exhausted trek home every night to her baby in Wilson Road, christened 'Black Alley' from the bricks thick with railway soot, the ceaseless clattering hum of Euston Station echoing through the walls. Her precious little boy kept clean in her well-scrubbed bedsit, the lingering odour of sour milk from the weary slattern with three ailing daughters next door.

The unwanted leers at work, from both foreman and supervisor. The brushing hands, the idle gropes in passing. Head washer at seventeen. Forewoman at twenty. All for just thirteen shillings a week stuck inside all day, every dreary hour marked by the mournful toll of the factory bell.

'It ain't fair!' she bursts out, her voice a squawk of outrage. 'It ain't *right!* Posh blokes getting treated like they're better than us just 'cause they're men, even though they don't cook or clean or … or do *anything*.'

She clenches her fists, seething with newfound passion. 'It's like in the Bible, innit? When that son comes home, the prodigal son, and he's been lazing around and wasting away his inheritance and spent all his money, and his dad gets a whole bleedin' party wheeled out just fer him.' Her voice has coarsened into a thick rough Cockney twang, her words sharp and bitter. 'And the other son, who's

136

been trying hard and slaving away and done everything what he's supposed to do, has to stand by and watch while his spendthrift brother gets a proper fancy dinner. All for doing *nuffin'!*'

She glares around at them, then blinks hard and blushes before groping for her seat, mumbling apologies. Rose watches her sit amid a wave of sympathetic murmurs, her bristling anger deflating and slowly seeping into the floor, and feels a familiar pang of smouldering resentment.

Men see things from a superior view, always gazing down as if on stilts; they don't realise how much easier it is for them to step over obstacles, or catch someone's eye across a crowded room, or keep safely out of the mud. The best of them might think they were seeing you eye to eye, but they never are, they're always peering down their noses at you, watching you mop and scrub and wash as if mopping and scrubbing and washing were the very worthwhile things that marked you out.

Men who own all legal rights over their wives' children. Men who control all their finances. Men who hold the deeds to their property. Men who slither through the corridors of power, while maids sweat in dingy basements and mill girls and servants toil away, condemned to relentless menial labour. Meanwhile the wives and daughters of gentlemen hold dutiful silence, condemned to do nothing meaningful except embroidery and idle parlour room smalltalk, their aspirations and hopes left to wither and rot. Their dreams stifled.

Until now.

Emma unrolls a map and spreads it on the table. 'Gather round, ladies. Everyone set for Friday, Molly? Good. Now, here's what we'll do ...'

All is prepared. Soon they'll gather in their hundreds, sisters for the cause, roaring with one voice. And if any policemen should intervene ...

Rose grips the Indian club in her handbag. She'll give them what for, by God. See how *they* like it!

The afternoon sun beats down as Rose turns onto Oxford Street. A hansom cab clatters past, and she forces herself not to shrink away, shield her face. Jenny is in school. Frank is busy painting some fancy mansion over in Knightsbridge. Both of them none the wiser. Better that way.

She pauses on the corner outside Lloyds Bank, her pockets heavy with stones. More and more women melt out of the passing crowd around her, sisters in arms arriving from all directions, watchful sentries taking up their positions facing the bank's large glass windows.

The pale afternoon air fizzles with coiled fury.

Emma's gloved fist punches the air.

'Votes for women!'

A shower of pebbles fly. *Crash!* A window shatters. Gloved fingers snap open handbags drawing out mallets, rolling pins, toffee hammers. *Smash!* Window after window shatters, shards of glass pouring onto the pavement. The crowd roars and surges forward, sweeping Rose along on a frenzied tide. Her sisters cheer as someone unfurls the tricoloured suffragette banner.

'Votes for Women!'

'Equal rights, equal voices!'

Police whistles shriek. Cheers trail off as the crowd turns, faltering, faces pale with dread …

A wall of mounted police block the road. Behind them horse-drawn police vans slew to a halt and more policemen flood out. Blocking the road.

Frozen silence, fragile as hair-thin glass …

'Charge!'

Whistles shriek as the mounted officers gallop forwards with a roar, the constables lunging at the nearest protesters.

CRACK. Rose crumples to the pavement. A stray stone skitters away over the cobbles. Thundering hooves clatter past her dazed eyes as the police charge scatters the demonstrators. A barricade of police officers shove through the disarrayed crowd, flailing about with their truncheons. The protestors wilt beneath the sudden brutal onslaught.

Rose staggers to her feet, panic and terror overwhelming her, cornered with the tightly-packed crowd kettled against the iron railings. Everywhere she sees carnage; burly officers throwing women half their size to the pavement, unarmed women beaten bloody into the pavement, their hands stamped on by hobnailed boots as they feebly crawl away. Truncheons slash down. Women are wrenched upright and manhandled towards the police vans. Emma is wrestled to the ground by an officer, Liz trapped in a headlock by another. A truncheon crashes against her temple and she crumples, blood streaking the cobblestones.

Where the hell is Molly?

Rose shoves through the panicked melee. Spies a nearby alleyway. Scrambles towards it.

'There's one!'

She hurries into the shadow of the alleyway, sagging against the slimy brick wall to catch her breath. Two hulking constables halt at the mouth of the alley, with drawn truncheons. They advance on her, scowling.

Wait ... wait ...

Her hand slips into her handbag, fingers closing around her concealed Indian club.

Now!

She shoves off the wall and charges them, swinging her handbag. One officer flinches back as the bag whips past his face, then doubles over as Rose's club cracks into his pudgy stomach. The other lumbers forward jabbing with his weapon, but Rose rounds on him, knocks his truncheon aside and bludgeons him with her handbag, sending him to the cobblestones.

Suddenly her arm is grabbed tight and she's yanked backward off balance. A third constable hangs from her elbow, wheezing and panting as his deadweight drags her back. She twists free and backhands him across the face, wood cracking bone, but a hand clamps her shoulder, pulling her off balance.

The other two stagger upright, spitting blood and glaring. One sinks a fist into her belly punching all breath from her lungs. She crumples to the ground, wheezing for air.

The blows rain down. She strikes back, lashing out furiously, heedless of pain and those hateful hands, but they fall on her again, three against one, three big brutal thugs with more strength, more clubs, more fists and boots, and soon she's overwhelmed. A truncheon rattles her skull. A steel-toed boot sinks into her ribs. The third scything blow brings her to her knees. She spits blood and struggles in vain as she's pinned down, hissing and spitting like a feral wildcat. Her arms are wrenched behind her back. Their rough groping hands pawing at her, dry fingers fumbling under her skirt, brushing her secret places where only Frank has ever dared caress –

Then she feels the awful click of a lock, the familiar cold bite of steel digging into her wrists. She goes still. No point in fighting handcuffs.

'Bitch,' snarls the bobby as he hauls her upright. His companions nurse their wounds, and Rose feels a vicious thrill of venom scorch through her; blood pours from one's nose, while the other cradles his injured arm and glares through a black eye.

She glimpses a flash of ginger curls through the crowd; Molly lolls groggily between two burly policemen, an ugly gash on her forehead as she's dragged by the hair towards a waiting Black Maria. Rose struggles as her captors bundle her roughly inside. Five blood-streaked faces gaze numbly from their steel-mesh cells. Like caged animals.

They're hurried through the streets, jolting from side to side as the police van rattles onward. Finally the crenelated ramparts of Royal Holloway loom above them, a bleak, foreboding place.

Every time she's shoved through these huge

oaken doors, Rose thinks, *this is it*. This is the day she'll have finally grown a thick skin to the smells, sights and sounds of this godforsaken prison.

And every single time, she's wrong. Her third incarceration yet, and there's still no hope of building an immunity to this hellhole. The sharp stinging tang of carbolic soap, the lingering sour stink of ammonia that claws the throat, wardresses' boots thumping on worn flagstones, steel doors clanging shut, a muffled cry, the faint stench of vomit wafting down the corridor and seeping through the walls. The hard stone floors that echo with shouts, cries, groans.

She dries up inside. Turns cold. Goes numb.

It turns out that if you have three cracked ribs, it really, really hurts to cry. So she doesn't.

She stands in line with three others, flinching as two female prison guards yank off her clothes. Her petticoats are roughly pulled off and dumped beside her jacket, coat and blouse. A third female warden scribbles notes of the clothing in a ledger, her pen scratching like a gnawing rat.

'One set of stockings,' she mutters, voice flat with boredom. 'Hole, right foot.'

Molly trembles with barely-repressed outrage, fists clenched. 'We're political prisoners. We have the right to wear our own clothes.' Another guard scoffs and tugs at her clothing, roughly trying to remove it. But Molly remains defiant, refusing to budge an inch. 'We have that right!'

The matron motions to Rose. 'Front and centre, girl. Now!' Rose edges forward, huddled in on herself, shielding her state of undress. She flinches as the matron grabs her goose-pimpled arm, forcing her around to face her fellow silent sentinels. 'Arms up. C'mon!' Her torn shawl finally falling loose leaving Rose stripped bare, fully exposed to her peers. She screws her eyes shut, naked and shivering as hot shame floods her cheeks. She breathes out. Forces her eyes open.

Not one of her sister suffragettes lets their gaze drift onto her nakedness. They all stare blankly ahead, daring the guards to try something, anything. Rose swallows back a sob of fierce pride at such an act of solidarity.

'Get dressed,' the matron sneers, dumping a loose bundle of clothes at her naked feet. The filthy grey knee-length smock, the drab brown blouse dotted with arrows, the woollen prison apron a pale shade of mustard. The mob cap that made even the prettiest face look like a peeled turnip. Rose forces down a shudder and slowly pulls on the rough, ill-fitting garments.

Sandwiched between two burly constables she's

frogmarched downstairs, slipping and stumbling on the grimy stone steps. Her arms are pinioned no matter how much she struggles and writhes. Grimy water pipes crawl across the unwashed walls. At the bottom they open a cell and shove her inside. The heavy steel door clangs shut behind her.

An empty stone cell. Four walls. No bucket. Just a low stone shelf to lie on. A plain metal chair. Not even an iron bedstead or barred window. A threadbare pillow, a slate-grey blanket. Above her, a naked bulb emits a soupy yellow glow, patches of black damp creeping across the walls. Nothing more. The second-division punishment cells, deep in the basement of Holloway.

It's the lack of windows; one always needs a glimpse of sky, however dismal grey, and a steady horizon on which to fix one's gaze. Outside the morning seeps into afternoon, fades into evening. But here? In her subterranean cell the weak electric light makes her feel purblind, isolated, severed from the outside world. You hear everything happening on all five floors, fifty-seven cells per floor, the snoring and the fights. All night. So she doesn't sleep much, her fitful prison dreams not of food or the warm comfort of home, but of shutters prised open, of dazzling sunlight spilling in.

A clock freckled brown with mould sits above the door, edging towards six. Its dull endless tick echoes through the cold interview room. Other scattered sounds dribble through the barred window; the distant clatter of iron-rimmed cartwheels, the impatient brassy squawk of a motorcar, the infantile whine of a cat in heat. Rose gazes at a swirling whorl in the tabletop, her blank dull-eyed mask hiding the seething anger within.

Rusty hinges squeal as the door opens. A thickset bearded man in brown tweed steps in and sits facing her. A brown envelope in his hand.

Rose's lip curls. 'Evening, Inspector Boyle. Don't want to keep you long. Not with all those rapists to catch and wife beaters to lock up.'

Boyle sighs heavily. 'Mrs Watts. Third time you've been inside these walls, isn't it, Rosemary?'

Rose scowls back. 'My friends call me Rose.'

'I'm sure they do.' Boyle steeples his fingers together and regards her coolly. 'Fifth arrest. Third time behind bars. You know why you're here.'

'Yes,' she mutters, the word emerging as a tiny flake of sound, like a crust of paint scratched from a wall. Her eyes flicker to the clock. 'I have to be home by six. My daughter. She'll need her tea.'

Boyle shakes his head. 'You won't be home for tea.' He glances down at her wedding ring. 'Want

146

me to contact your husband, Mrs Watts?'

Rose presses her trembling hands firmly in her lap, desperately trying to stem the rising panic. Boyle nods calmly, letting the silence hang, then: 'We picked up another activist just yesterday.' He huffs through his nose. 'Gutsy little firecracker. Two bricks hidden in her bloomers. Works for Mrs Pankhurst. I asked her why she does it.' His lips twitch in a grudging smile. 'She said it makes life worth living. I admire that. There's no madness in it. They know *exactly* what they're doing.' He meets her gaze again, voice hardening. 'But my opinion doesn't matter. My job is to enforce the law, Mrs Watts. So I'm going to give you some advice ... and I *sincerely* hope you take it.'

Rose holds his stare with quiet desperation, eyes stinging with furious tears as he continues, 'You'll serve time now. Three days, worst case. Then you'll walk free. Go home to your family. To your husband. In return –' he slides the envelope across, opens it, '– you will help me.'

Photographs. A dozen grainy black and white surveillance snapshots. Of her. Molly. Liz.

Rose meets his gaze, her resolve wavering as his voice rolls on smoothly: 'You have information for us. Anything you know or hear, even if only a snippet of conversation, it's of interest. When they meet. What they talk of …'

Her eyes slide away from his.

'Look at me.'

Her hands clench, nails digging into her palms. Finally she glances up. 'So that's all I am to you, is it? Your pretty little informer?'

Boyle's nostrils flare. 'Now look here –'

'Sod you! I ain't no damn snitch!' She glares back, fuming with indignation. 'We do what we must because men won't *listen!* Just feeble old men telling us to mind our manners. Know our place. They won't grant us a seat at the table, so we'll *make* them see reason.'

Boyle shakes his head. 'And why couldn't you just *ask* for it? Like normal people?'

'We tried that! At public meetings!' A seething rage rises inside her, bubbling up from within. 'We asked Cabinet Ministers to change the law, and their stewards dragged us out. They punched us, kicked us, manhandled us like common drunkards. So yes. Of course we changed tactics. We had to.'

Boyle snorts. 'What, like smashing windows? Hardly proper behaviour –'

'Hang what's proper!' Rose bristles with indignation. 'You want me to respect the law? Then make the law respectable! All we want is an equal voice, is that too much to ask?'

Boyle rubs his temples. 'D'you really think anyone *listens* to militants like you? That anyone cares? They don't. You're nothing to them. I've seen plenty like you. People who sacrificed life for a vengeful cause. I *know* your type. So do they. Girls without good money, without prospects that want things to improve. Easy to hook you, reel you in. They primp and pamper you and say you're footsoldiers of some noble cause. But you're only meat for a useless struggle you won't win.'

He takes out a business card and presses it into her hand. 'I'm offering you a lifeline. For the sake of your family. For your daughter.' Rose glances down at her feet, the card crumpled in her fist.

'Take it,' Boyle insists. 'Before it's too late.'

The iron-studded prison gate groans open, and Rose, Molly and Laura totter out into dazzling sunshine, pale-faced, battered and weakened. But still standing.

A welcome reception of elegant ladies greet them with bouquets, their faces creased with pride. Frank waits nearby; Rose staggers into his arms with a groan of relief. 'Frank …'

'Came as soon as I heard,' he murmurs. 'C'mon. Let's get you home.'

The elegant suffragettes beam at her. One of

149

them hands a posy of flowers to Laura, then takes out a silver Holloway brooch and pins it to her lapel. 'Everyone gets one their first incarceration.'

Then she pulls Molly and Rose close, her voice a hushed undertone. 'Rest assured, the escalation of violence from the police *will* be met with force. You'll receive your instructions.'

She clasps their hands fiercely, eyes shining.

'For the cause!'

Feeble dawn sunlight peeks over the rooftops as Rose hurries towards a pillar box. After glancing up and down the street, she slips her slender hand through the metal mouth. First a letter. Then she feeds in a parcel wrapped in a paraffin-soaked rag, lighting the fuse and shoving it inside. Her heart hammers against her ribs as she turns away, hurrying to a bicycle leaning nearby.

An almighty bang behind her. She flinches but mounts up, begins cycling away. Halfway down the street she glances back.

The pillar box is a blasted ruin behind her, thick smoke pouring out. Flames lick hungrily skyward. Blown high into the air, fragments of charred letters drift to earth like freshly fallen snow, fluttering in the breeze. Shrouding the pavement in white.

Rose looks ahead, smiling.

She slumps back in the chair, picking at her nails.

They'd cornered her on the way home. Surrounded her, cuffed her and dragged her into a police van. Brought her back here again, to the same cold interview room. The same faint echoes of freedom beyond the high barred window.

The door creaks open and Boyle enters, the Daily Mirror in one hand. He approaches the table staring down at the headline, glances her way then takes the opposite chair, shaking his head sadly.

He slaps down the paper; ANARCHY IN THE UK screams the headline. LONDON POSTBOXES TARGETED. PANKHURST FACES PRISON.

Boyle pinches the bridge of his nose. 'Your old firecracker's taken the rap for this, hasn't she? She'll milk every ounce of press sympathy from behind bars.'

Rose stares leadenly back, steely and unafraid. A twinkle of grudging respect in Boyle's creased face. 'You ladies sure cleaned yourselves up well. We couldn't find a scrap of explosives on any of you.'

Rose shrugs, feigning nonchalance. 'Then why am I here?'

Boyle steeples his hands together, frowning. 'Oh, you'll be charged with illegal meetings if nothin' else. Inciting civil unrest. Vandalism.

Conspiracy. Plenty enough to make your life hell.' He lets the fraying silence stretch almost to snapping point, then: 'Y'know a housemaid was on her way when the bomb blew? Forgot to post a letter, poor girl. If she'd arrived just two minutes later ...' he shrugs, '... what would *that*'ve done for your righteous cause? Hm?' He sighs heavily. 'Violence doesn't discern. It swallows everyone, both innocent and guilty. Whatever gave you the right to put that woman's life at risk?'

Rose glares back. 'What gave *you* the right to watch women beaten bloody, then turn a blind eye and do *nothing?* You're a damn hypocrite –'

'I uphold the law.'

'That's bollocks to me!' The bitterness in her voice would have soured milk. She leans forward, eyes glistening with defiance. 'Why should I care? I'm worth no less than you, but I've had no say in making it – *none!*'

Boyle shakes his head wearily. 'That's just an excuse, the law's all we have. And you bloody lawbreakers –'

'We break things. We burn things.' Her voice rises as a fierce rush of pride floods through her. 'We smash and bomb because War's the only language that men ever listen to. We tried talking, and you shouted us down. We tried signs and placards and peaceful protests, and you clubbed us and trampled us with horses. *That*'s why. 'Cause you've beaten us and betrayed us and lied to us and there's *nothing else left!*'

A ringing silence falls. Boyle gazes coolly back at her. 'Then there's nothing left but to stop you.'

She leans forward, her voice low and vehement. 'What're you gonna do, huh? *Lock us all up?* We're in every home, we're half the human race.' She leans back, eyes burning with defiance. 'You can't stop us all!'

Boyle picks at his sleeve 'And if you starve yourself? We'll just force-feed you.'

Rose smiles back. 'Go ahead. But we *will* win.'

The hours crawl by down here, shuttered off from the outside world. She lapses into a fitful doze, only awakening moments later to the gruel bowl pushed through the door hatch. She turns over to face the wall, her bruised belly groaning in protest.

'Piss off.'

The spyhole grate scrapes open through the night. From outside, countless church bells chime the hour. Their discordant melody echoes in her ears as she huddles on her freezing stone bed.

Just after six. Frank will be wondering where she

is. He'll glance up at the clock, peer out into the gloomy street and scratch his head. 'Where's your Ma?' he'll ask Jenny, tickling her ribs as she giggles. 'What's she fetchin' for supper?'

Wheels squeak outside. The clatter of an approaching feeding trolley, the purposeful footsteps of the doctor and wardresses growing louder, almost deafening. She braces herself.

The trolley stops outside. Keys rattle in the lock. She grits her teeth and stands. The cell door swings inward, rusty hinges screaming. She sees the large bowl atop the trolley, the heavy jug of milk. The brown coil of rubber tubing. The burly wardresses flanking the doctor like an honour guard. At once they storm inside and overpower her, shoving her into the chair, her arms firmly pinned down.

The doctor approaches, the rubber tube hanging from his hand. Rose's head is wrenched back. The doctor gazes down impassively. 'Five days without food,' he murmurs. 'Will you eat now?'

Silence. He nods to the others. 'Hold her still.'

Rose writhes and thrashes, moaning as the doctor shoves the nozzle of rubber tubing up her nostril. She gags and whimpers. Her legs kick, defiant.

The tube is rammed further and further in, the doctor steadily feeding it through his hands. He nods to the wardress who passes over the funnel and milk jug. Begins to pour. Rose's vision blurs as the milk splashes into the funnel. Trickling down the tube. Burning pain floods her nose, she's choking, suffocating, drowning –

Wham! One of her flailing feet boots the jug of milk out of the wardress's hands, slamming it against the wall. Milk splatters the floor. The wardress jerks back, staring down at her dripping hands.

'Bitch!' she snarls.

Rose snarls back, gulping a ragged desperate lungful of air. The doctor retrieves the jug. Continues pouring. She struggles like a chained wildcat. No use. The milk creeps down the tube. Blinding, searing pain rips through her.

Her vision blurs. Her mind detaches itself, untethered and floating adrift in a vast endless churning sea. Now she's standing outside her own precious flat, peering through the murky glass into a dining room bathed in warm candlelight. Frank and Jenny sit together at the dinner table, safely snug behind their own front door, tucking eagerly into ham and eggs. Safe and warm.

She blinks. The vision shrivels away; she is here, underground, surrounded, trapped and immobile under uncaring hands, choking and gagging while

155

her jaw clenches and her fingernails prick her palms and icy milk burns down her throat.

Her fight for voting rights won't change the world, won't usher in a new golden age of equality. The right to vote won't lift women out of dreary, dangerous dead-end jobs in factories and laundries, won't pay them a decent wage, won't free them from being trapped in loveless marriages, won't stamp out the threat of abuse and rape by their fathers, husbands, brothers and bosses. Won't change anything worthwhile, really.

But a rising tide of reckoning is coming. A million voices all across the nation now roaring aloud with one mighty voice: *No more.* A united mass of female might from all walks of life – politicians' wives, grandmothers, committee members, letter writers, hecklers and militants. All activists. All sisters to the cause. All suffragettes fighting for a better future, a brave new world where every newborn girl will have a far brighter future than theirs. A future that she helped force, even here, trapped and force-fed in an underground room, her single flickering flame of defiance wavering against the overwhelming dark.

But a win is a win, no matter how small.

These walls may swallow her screams.

But never her spirit.

BUTCHER

Jack Lark sips his pint of beer and sets it back on the counter with a wistful sigh. It'll have to last him all evening. He doesn't mind, really; it's the slow company in the Grey Horse that he likes.

Bill Weaver the barman leans over the counter. 'I could top that pint up for you, Jack. On the house, no charge?'

Jack smiles and shakes his head. 'Cheers, Bill, but no thanks. Everyone's going without these days. We're all in this war for the long haul; if we don't tighten our belts and pull together for England, we may as well let the Germans march down Piccadilly tomorrow.' He combs his fingers through thinning black hair, already greying at the edges. 'Besides, I'm on duty later; wouldn't do if the villagers saw their local bobby rolling around drunk, would it?'

The barman chuckles. 'Fair enough, mate.'

The door creaks open. A chilly draught swirls into the bar as a stranger hurries inside. His dark hair is greased flat to a thin skull, shrewd bloodshot eyes darting around the room. He cradles a brown wax paper parcel under one arm.

'Evening, sir,' Bill smiles, 'and what can I get you?'

'Nuffin,' the stranger croaks. He jabs a grubby finger at his parcel. 'S'more a case of what I can get *you*!'

'A case of whisky would be nice.'

'Nah!' the young man scowls. He glances warily at Jack then beckons for Bill to join him over in a quiet corner. Although he mutters in that low, hoarse voice, Jack can still overhear most of his words: 'Nice bit o' beef … fresh as a daisy … ten shillings!'

The barman shrugs. 'No ration coupons.'

'Nah! Don't need none. Nice bit o' beef. Cook it up. Serve beef sandwiches to the regulars, eh? Just nine shillings to yer, guv!'

Bill sniffs in disdain. 'Probably dog meat.'

'Heh! I'll give yer dog meat. Killed just down the road, only this mornin'. Fresh as a daisy!' The stranger's red-rimmed eyes narrow. 'I can sell this fer twice the price in London, mate!'

'Then good luck to you.' Bill smiles coolly, and turns away to polish a glass.

'Yer'll be sorry!' the stranger snarls, glares over

at Jack then scuttles out the door.

Bill meets the eyes of his old friend. 'Heard all that, Jack?'

'Every word, Bill.'

'Surprised you didn't arrest him.'

'I'm not in me uniform yet … besides, I'm more interested to find out who's supplying this mystery meat.'

Bill rubs his stubbled chin – new razors are hard to come by these days. 'My money's on those Wades; a shifty family if ever I saw one.'

'Then I'll start there,' Jack promises. 'If I'm not back by twelve, call the station, won't you? Cheers.' He drains the last of his beer, pulls on his coat and sets off home to change into his uniform.

Jack wheels his bicycle down the slippery lane towards Trent Marsh Farm. Blackout curfew has already begun; the thin slit in his front lamp shroud shows almost no light ahead, and the faint moon is little help. The constable curses as he slithers along the rutted track, ankle-deep in mud, overhanging branches snatching at his helmet. Fifty-nine in March – so much for that distant retirement dream!

The farm gate is slimy with moss as he pushes it open. No lights glow from the farmhouse windows – Jack would have been angry if he'd seen any.

Some of these farmers are so careless about blackout rules. They know the Air Raid Precaution wardens would never venture this far out into the freezing damp night, away from their cosy firesides.

He shivers at the memory: a warm night in May. Searchlights slicing the moonlit, cloudless sky. The relentless droning buzz of enemy bombers high overhead, like a vengeful swarm of angry hornets. Their endless buzz mingled with the wailing howl of air raid sirens, the distant shuddering boom of falling incendiary bombs. Searing heat washing over his face as he struggled with the spluttering fire hose, other firefighters scrambling over mounds of rubble, desperately trying to quench the raging firestorm. No barrage balloons. No anti-air cannons. Nothing to do but endure beneath the withering onslaught, planes swooping low and unmolested, stitching lines of dust up and down the street from their machine-gunners. Flames licking hungrily from gutted buildings. A half-mile column of fire engulfing Fore Street and High Street.

And the screams. Dear God, the *screams*.

More than a hundred and sixty dead. Forty-seven fireguards who never made it home.

He breathes out. Blinks away the images, and presses onward.

He props his bike against the farmhouse wall, unhooks his lamp and shines it through the frosty window. No shutters or curtains. It's deserted, silent and cold. But no hay or straw in any corner of the large barn. Odd.

In the field behind the farmhouse stands a haystack shrouded under a waterproof cover. Nothing here to suggest an illicit slaughterhouse.

He stumbles against an oil drum with a dull clang and rubs his aching knee, cursing the darkness. Then he falls silent; the nighttime blindness is now his greatest ally. Although he can see almost nothing his ears are sharpened. And his sense of smell. *Follow your nose, Jack*, his father had always told him. *You'll sniff out trouble quicker that way.*

Owls wail in the distant woods. Unseen rats scuttle in the barn. And another faint noise from behind the empty building. Someone is sawing. Jack strains his ears and creeps along the haystack. The soft sawing isn't the soft cutting of wooden logs. No – the brittle sawing of bones he's always overheard passing the butcher's shop.

The sawing stops. Muffled voices, then a harsh staccato chopping. Jack edges along the side of the haystack and peers around the corner. The wafer-thin moon illuminates the field, silvering every blade of grass. It's empty!

Now the sawing echoes from *behind* him. He hurries back along the haystack, turns the corner and gazes out into the deserted farmyard. *What now? Ghosts?* Jack is almost ready to hurry back to his bicycle and pedal the hell out of here. Then a loud, ugly laugh barks from his left. From the haystack.

No … *inside* the stack.

Using his lamp he carefully retraces his steps, treading softly along the haystack, feeling blindly until his fingers scrape hard wooden boards. Hay bales have been piled high against the walls of a wooden outhouse to disguise it. But he soon finds the hidden door and slips inside.

The glaring oil lamps make him squint as he steps inside from the frosty November night. The sickly-sweet stench of freshly spilled blood is overpowering.

But most appalling are the three pairs of flinty eyes turned upon him.

Farmer Wade holds a large meat axe. Each son clutches a dripping carving knife.

'Evenin', Constable,' Wade grunts. His stony face cracks into a wide smile, baring crooked yellow teeth. 'Come fer your share, 'ave you?'

Jack Lark's eyes drift over the pink, naked,

blood-spattered carcasses. 'Have you a license to slaughter and sell these livestock?'

The taller son swaggers forward. 'Don't need one. These animals are casualties, see? P'raps you'd like a nice steak … free of charge, of course.' The knife twists in his blood-streaked hands, flashing under the lamplight.

'That cow couldn't walk.' The second son smirks. 'We had to put her down.' His fingers drum along the knife handle.

The Special Constable's mouth tightens. 'And these two calves?' *Watch those knives, careful, keep watching the knives …*

'Motherless.' Farmer Wade shrugs. 'Poor beasts had to die.'

'That looks like a pig – don't tell me the cow was his mother too!'

'No, it was old, lame … Believe me, Constable!'

'Funny – I don't. Let's see if a jury at Exeter Crown Court will believe your claptrap, shall we?'

Wade's face flushes red. 'One more death won't make any difference,' he growls.

'Might as well be hanged for a cop as a pig,' his taller son mutters, and steps towards the policeman with his knife rising. 'Nobody'll ever know what happened to you!'

Jack's hand drifts to the truncheon at his belt.

'Careful with that, laddie. Interfering with a policeman's a prison offence.' He draws his weapon, its hefty weight a reassuring comfort. 'Real dark night out there – you might fall down and hurt yourself. Cracked ribs. Broken skull.'

The farmer's son scowls, eyeing the stout oaken club. 'You wouldn't dare, old man.'

'After being threatened with knives? Watch me.' Jack forces a calm smile, despite his churning stomach. 'Bill Weaver down the pub knows where I am. He'll call the police station if I'm not back by midnight.'

'Yer bluffing,' the other son sneers.

'Young bloke, London accent, greasy black hair. Came into the Grey Horse tonight and tried to sell some meat. *Your* meat. If you know who I'm talking about then you know I'm telling the truth.'

'An' if we don't?' Farmer Wade bares yellow teeth. 'Yer a dead man. You ain't got nuffin'.'

Jack Lark shrugs. 'Not quite.' The solid hefty truncheon smacks down into his palm. 'I have *this*.'

For a long moment the only sound is the hissing of the oil lamps and the distant owls wailing. Finally Farmer Wade runs his thumb along the blade of his axe and smiles. 'Only trying to make a living, Constable. Only trying to make a living!'

About the Author

Half Welsh, half Brummie, and terrible at both accents, Tom Burton has lived in Nigeria, Oman and the Netherlands. He currently lives and writes with his family in Devon, his imagination nourished by the magic of dark chocolate and Yorkshire Tea.

His short stories have featured in numerous online journals including *Spillwords Press*, *Literally Stories*, *Dreaming in Fiction* and *Whatever Keeps the Lights On*.

Only Human is his third self-published collection of short stories, after *Wildlands* (nature fiction, 2020) and *Pocketful of Time* (historical fiction, 2021). Visit his website to find out more:

www.slumdogsoldier.wordpress.com

Printed in Great Britain
by Amazon